# WHITE JADE

# WHITE JADE

## AND OTHER STORIES

## ALEX KUO

2008 •
La Grande, Oregon •

WORDCRAFT OF OREGON
LLC

## Also by Alex Kuo

*The Window Tree*
*New Letters from Hiroshima and Other Poems*
*Changing the River*
*Chinese Opera*
*Lipstick and Other Stories*
*This Fierce Geography*
*Panda Diaries*

*This book is for Katherine, for my first words.*

*With thanks to the Rockefeller Foundation for a Bellagio residency, and Gianna Celli for her gracious support.*

# Acknowledgements

Grateful acknowledgement is extended to the editors of *amerasia journal, Ploughshares* and *Post Road* in which earlier versions of "10,000 Dildoes," "Free Kick," and "The Lunch" first appeared.

ISBN: 978-1-877655-61-6
LCN: 2008928198

First Edition, October 2008

Published by
Wordcraft of Oregon, LLC
P.O. Box 3235
La Grande, OR 97850
www.wordcraftoforegon.com
info@wordcraftoforegon.com

Text design by David Memmott
Cover design by Kristin Summers (www.redbatdesign.com)
Author photo by Zoe Filipkowska

Printed in the United States of America

# CONTENTS

# 10,000 DILDOES

*For Wen Ho Lee*

T he Hisatsinoms must have marveled at these vague purple flowers, at this elevation and distance maybe sego lily or spurred lupine or mountain aster until their need to know in Diné. Balanced on the palm of this land six-hundred years ago children standing around waiting anxiously while their parents dug up its bulbs, peeled and juicy and oh so sweet. Or later, as survival food for immigrants facing drought and locusts not more than a hundred-years ago. Or for this newer immigrant standing at this Valle Grande roadstop, did he dig one up—lily or lupine or aster without the English adjectives—this research scientist from the Los Alamos National Lab just down the hill to the north, this Professor Li Fangzhi, or did he not because picking here was now against the law? Maybe he just stood there drenched in their same expansive sunlight under the bluest of skies and imagined another space within this massive volcanic caldera.

He stuck around and waited a moment longer looking into the shade of the distant Redondo Peak at the top of the continent. In the meantime more cars have stopped—licenses from Pennsylvania, Connecticut and always Illinois—along with their digital cameras and bottled water and fanny packs. His peripherals were plugged in, just waiting for some maniac to come along and turn this into Literature—dodging evil husbands and jeopardized wives along the way, the state patrol, and raising questions about the culture of language, social responsibility, art, and aha, the short story itself.

Li didn't often leave his apartment for more than the few minutes it took to walk to the post office to pick up his mail or the grocery store, except when he went to the office or his mahjong club. But early this evening he was doing both, picking up some bulk peanuts and mini-pretzels on sale before sauntering back across the Furrs parking lot to the

Los Alamos Mahjong Parlor tucked into the mini-mall where a player, friend and LANL-colleague and fellow physicist had waved to him, first from a distance too far for his eyesight.

"Here, let me help you with those bags," One-arm Bandit offered when Li was close enough. They called Issie that because he played faster using only his left hand than almost every player in New Mexico who used both, and that was almost everyone, including Li. At least it's better than *Leftie*.

"Thank you." Li handed him the Furrs plastic bags and fumbled for his keys in his windbreaker. "It's nice this evening, this Daylight Savings Time gives us. A spectacular sunset."

The two of them took a moment to shade their eyes to look southwest at the fading sunset behind the Jemez Mountains, before turning around and opening the double glass doors of the club.

"Quite different than Waltham or Cambridge or New York City, I would imagine," One-arm Bandit reminded Li.

Yes, first a Nieman from Harvard, then a year at Princeton before another at Columbia and then Brandeis, four years wasted doing absolutely nothing. "You're quite correct. You went to MIT, you must know. And you must know too, Issie, my friend," he continued, "before that I was hiding in a locked cubbyhole inside the U.S. Embassy in Beijing for a year before getting smuggled out. But I was lucky, that was not as severe as that group of evangelical Pentecostals in the basement of the American Embassy in Moscow for five years, or that cleric dissident, Cardinal Joseph Mindszenty in Budapest for fifteen."

"Yes, so, Li, are you going to bring up the Albuquerque tournament tonight," One-arm Bandit asked, looking up at the events calendar in the freshly painted small kitchen area and filling the commercial coffee maker with water.

"Yes, the one in July." Li was counting the tables that needed to be set up for a Saturday night game, the week's biggest, and bringing out the same number of surplus, wool, Forest Service blankets to cover them. There had been several noise complaints from the other two occupants of this wing of the mall, a combination yoga exercise center and health food store, and an up-scale, gentle chiropractic office decorated with Beverly Doolittle prints. To dampen the loud cracking sound of mahjong tiles hitting the wooden table in a dramatic pong or kong, they had insisted, but for Li, without that noise it's not the same game.

"Forty or sixty?"

Li hesitated a moment, laying out the mahjong boxes and arranging two sets of numbers in his head simultaneously. "Yes, sixty, thank you." No need to be cheap here. The members are happy and playing well, many twice a week, and some more. And more are showing up for both the beginner and intermediate lessons as well, even though their playing level is the same.


Yes, people thought he was doing quite well here, after his career move from Brandeis to LANL. He was fed up sitting around doing nothing on those fancy, political asylum fellowships, with its catered finger-food lunches and sherry colloquia. Wanting to get off this academic welfare program, he surfed the NET and found the opening at LANL. With his cachet of Harvard-Princeton-Columbia-Brandeis-1600 Pennsylvania Avenue recommendations, even the University of California that operates LANL could not turn down his application. Truth be told, his work at this lab has nothing to do with his fancy degrees in astrophysics, though at the lunchrooms they debate what all astrophysics includes. But that seems to be an issue in another life altogether, not Professor Li's. He had been euchred by the damn FBI security clearance test, removed from doing any sensitive work at all, not even in the remote galaxial cosmology of astrophysics—they thought he was a heathen Chinee. What irony! Hired, but can't be fired—tenured, but not allowed to do anything more than maintain the fancy duplicating machines and linked printers!

So, his vetted job description here did not include pursuing either side of the Kennedy question—Ask not what physics can do for you, but what you can do for physics. Fortunately that also meant he did not have to travel the high school science or public university commencement speaking circuits because they thought his English and his teeth were not good enough, and for this he was thankful.

So what can a recent immigrant and political dissident of Tiananmen Square do in Los Alamos, New Mexico, in the middle of the George Bush I presidency? What can a physicist without portfolio or flag do, that is, besides going to his office five days a week and re-routing the in-house organizational documents and re-ordering the e-mail prompts, tasks normally relegated to the lower order engineers? Open another Chinese restaurant with a green card? Start a contract bridge club? He had been told that when the partnership of Leo Storm and Joel Oppenheimer left town in the late 1940s when LANL was temporarily downsized, the community's interest in bridge evaporated, along with the thousands of subscriptions to *Popular Mechanics* and *Sunset Magazine*. No way! Then he thought, Hey, why not, Jews, mahjong, Jews and mahjong. Sorry kiddo, but there you have it—he opened a mahjong club!

We have to organize the trip to the Albuquerque tournament tonight, Li reminded himself when he was stalled at a pedestrian crossing in his rumpled baseball jacket, tempted to take the illegal plunge and violate the blinking DONT WALK sign half a block from a U.S. Post Office. It'll be the same discussion as last year's: some will want to take the slow, winding mountain road, but one with a view; and others the faster Interstate by way of Santa Fe. Either way, a compromise will be reached, Highway 4 going down in the morning, and I-25 back at night, same as last year.

Then he will ride in someone's backseat on the drive south in the morning, looking out the window into the blurred, flat sweep of ponderosas and kicked-aside road kill, an occasional arroyo squinting my pupils into focus, and of course, the mandatory pause at the Valle Grande or Baca Ranch roadstop at the top of the 8,200' pass just to keep the maniac's story straight, same as last year. And on their way back the next evening after the tournament, he will have to listen to another cultural discussion on changing the rules of mahjong to make the movement clockwise, to make the game more natural and friendly for Americans. He would then have to ignore the conversation and look out the window into the night of skeletal pump jacks bobbing for imagined oil in every section of this land that's just dry enough but not caked and cracked enough to shatter anyone's illusions.

When Li got to the post office and unlocked his mailbox, he was surprised to find six pink slips on top of the couple of bills that had arrived over the weekend, his usual mail. Six packages? Usually the scoring supplies from the American Mah Jong Association came in one small carton—but six!

"You have six boxes here," the postal clerk with the name *Larry* on a burnished nameplate above his shirt pocket explained, his extended arms illustrating their size to the physicist. "You'll need a car for them."

"Okay—I'll bring a friend back this afternoon," Li said, still puzzled. "Where are they from," he asked, pushing his glass frames back.

"They're from China, Shanghai, I believe."

When the shipment arrived in San Francisco two weeks ago, it mustered serious U.S. Postal Service hesitation when the manifest labeled ADULT TOYS was grimly noticed. The six boxes had passed inspection with reservation, not opened only because the San Francisco office, unlike Western Union and IT&T, had a long tradition of political neutrality to maintain—it did not open other people's mail, not even at the continual insistence of the FBI or DoD, even during wartime. We saw those same packages next at the Los Alamos Post Office where One-arm Bandit and Li pulled up in Issie's car that afternoon to collect that which had survived both the Pacific journey and postal inspection.

The first thing Professor Li exclaimed in Chinese when the first box was finally opened and its contents spilled onto the floor was roughly *fu manchu*, which, loosely translated into English meant Holy Shit or Holy Moly, whichever came first. One-arm Bandit and Li had been at it at the mahjong club for several cautious minutes unwrapping layer after layer with scissors, packing knife and teeth, peeling away sheets of cheesecloth, waxed paper, string with dead knots and sealing wax.

"What is it," One-arm Bandit asked, looking at the pink, plastic object in Li's hand that resembled some projectile, rocket, nuclear submarine, or penis.

There were more—in firm plastic or pliable latex, in all shapes and sizes and colors of bubble gum and jelly beans, this one smooth plastic in pink and black, another in ribbed latex resembling some giant sea slug—in all, hundreds of them, no, thousands of them.

"These are dildoes," One-arm Bandit finally said, laughing, "direct from Shanghai. Li, you have a secret life you've been hiding from us, or are you planning to open a sex toys store in this mall or what?"

"I don't know anything about them. I never ordered," Li stammered, but he was more curious about how they worked. "Double-A batteries," he added, pointing upwards.

"What's that?"

"In the top drawer behind you, some double-A batteries," Li waved.

But they could not make any of them work—double checking the positive and negative connections and confirming the contacts—not even after trying out several different ones, pink and green, plastic and latex, small and extra-large, and mixing them.

"Something's wrong here, none of them works, maybe a flaw in the automated soldering. No quality check in Shanghai."

"No matter," Li added. "We're physicists, remember? We must be able to make these simple gadgets work."

"But who, who sent them to you? Who in Shanghai has your post office address?"

"I don't know. Nobody. I don't know."

"You think someone is trying to compromise you, put attention on you?"

"What?" Li looked up, letting a pink one drop back into a box.

One-arm Bandit offered his paranoiac suspicion. Beijing wanted weapons secrets from LANL, but it knew better than to recruit a Chinese or a Jew, too obvious—it'll go after some white bread physicist with two first names, a Robert Frank or Timothy James, as difficult as they may be to locate at LANL, or the rest of New Mexico. Then the Ministry of Counter-Intelligence exploited this idea to create a scapegoat, a surrogate who'll divert attention away from the real spy. Smear a Chinese herring red and the operation will take care of itself in the American intelligence industry still hooked on the Cold War view of the world. Throw these ham-fisted pukes a little reverse psychology, ha, ha, set up a special effects operation, put a patsy into a mission impossible, and the wish would take its course.

Then the two of them talked of unfamiliar things in a low familiar voice, as though their words, however small and however conjectural, were putting the world in place. And they were, they were in the place inside the place inside the place.

In reality, they were at risk inside this place, at least Professor Li Fangzhi was. Nothing came in or went out of Los Alamos that was not recorded by the National Security Agency satellites, whether by snail mail or e-mail, truck, plane or bicycle, telephone or semaphore. And it had tracked the movement of these six boxes from Shanghai to Los

Alamos and identified their recipient. LANL got this kind of security coverage because of its role in weapons development, although the University of California preferred to call it defense research. The Trident and Minuteman warheads were designed here, as well as the depleted-uranium rockets' red glare, and this was the only remaining facility still producing weapons grade plutonium pits in the U.S., at fifty a year.

Regional lore shook at the sins committed at LANL, suspected groceries at Los Alamos cost two to three times more than the rest of New Mexico, and predicted that the radiated trees around it can only be purged by fire. It recent summers during the anniversary of the bombing of Hiroshima and Nagasaki on August 6/9, out-of-towners gathered in the city's parks for several days to protest against such weapons development—physicists, housewives, high school kids, vegetarians, cabbies, Wes Studi. They used everything against the fascists who preached nationalism and national security—soil and bone, root and blood, song and leaf.

Li could tell that his phones were beginning to emit strange noises and pauses in the middle of conversations, both at his apartment and the mahjong club. His PC was inexplicably losing files and skipping functions. Some of his colleagues at the office were beginning to avoid him. Last Tuesday he was turned away at the security gate and instructed to go to the Badge Office for a new identity card to hang from his neck.

But the mahjong players were supportive and had a sense of humor about this. One-arm Bandit gave Li an article on Eros, a clitoral suction pump awaiting F.D.A. clearance, and someone else asked with a wink if he knew anything about vasodilators and hormone patches. Still another suggested that Li apply for funding to attend a conference organized and funded by Pfizer, the manufacturer of Viagra.

Get on a Boeing 747, but where to?

Professor Li was being watched, and not just by us. Even the fortune cookies that appeared with the check at the end of his meals in Asian restaurants have been examined, especially those left uncracked at the table. Ah, the ever diabolical Chinese, encrypting and transmitting messages inside fortune cookies in full view of the public—this one distributed by Super K, with a panda bear icon, and it can be ordered from Kari-Out Co., NY, 1-800-433-8799. And some of these fortunes contained sets of lucky numbers that can mean anything. Definitely more subtle than the encrypted messages spelled out under or above marked letters in a copy of the Bible, or *The Dream of the Red Chamber* in English.

But Professor Li was not laughing about this—it's his life that's at risk here. He was thinking about getting on another 747, this time to cross the Atlantic. One-arm Bandit had been telling him about the American WW II bomber pilot Garry Davis who had renounced his citizenship in 1948 and moved to a farm near Basel, the town where France, Germany and Switzerland converged in a complex of geographic and political ambiguities. There he'd declared himself a citizen of the world and, citing the United Nations Declaration of Human Rights that said a political entity does not have to be a nation-state to issue passports and that passports are to be used for travel identification purposes only, began issuing passports that were at least honored by India, Vietnam and the Vatican. I can find this farm, I can, Professor Li said to himself. I can get a passport there and start living my life again without politics.

Oh, hell, that kind of escape won't work at all—it didn't back in the 50s, and will less likely now. The fortune from tonight's cookie sparked a clue: *One old friend is better than two new ones.* It told Professor Li to reverse the brain drain and go back to China and do weapons research for Norinco. But that won't work either, damn it, since the government there is less interested in cloning the American W-88 multiple-warhead ICBM than putting its proven AK-47s in the hands of every teenager on earth, with or without ammunition. It's also obvious that since Professor Li haven't done any physics for more than three decades, counting those years cobbled in political rehabilitation and later as vice-president of CUS&T, same thing, he would have to do something else for his day job.

Last Sunday's local newspaper copped an AP story about Shanghai pharmaceuticals producing fake Viagra, even duplicating Pfizer's patented blue diamond-shape. Professor Li thought just maybe he could find a distant, entrepreneurial cousin in Shanghai who can make the connection between these factories and the party that sent him those boxes of dildoes and provide an introduction. He had an idea they won't be able to turn down. It will make them millions! Didn't Deng Xiaoping say "To be rich is glorious"?

He'll design a new dildo in the shape of a pistol, and just to show he had assimilated some Los Alamos culture, it'll be called the Cowboy Dildo or the Erotic Gunslinger. Its hammer will serve as the On/Off switch, and the trigger will control its vibration speed. The marketing staff can describe it as Cocked and Ready, Load Up with Double-As and You're Ready to Rock, Take Control of Your Fantasies. It'll flood the global market. Didn't the Little Emperor also say that it didn't matter if the cat was white or black, as long as it caught the mouse? Dang it, that's it, that's it!

The necessity to resolve his life with such barre logic! He couldn't switch it off any more than the maniac. So much for what we think, can you imagine! If Professor Li can still dance after this tangled story without taking a debilitating blow to the head, what about the rest of us, pressed as we are against the language of this imagined story, word by word?

# REGRETS ONLY

There are several ways to produce a written record of what happened in those two weeks in March, 2001, at Hainan Island. But for Seymour, maybe there's only one. Approach the story without clunky embellishments and capitulations to political shortcuts, however tempting and time saving, because he believed that what's overlooked will not leave us alone and often come back through some encrypted backdoor in our least expected moment—like in a dream—to trick us and deposit a metaphor we are about to understand, but regretfully never quite do.

So then, it began on their return flight to Kadena on that March, cirrus and dreamlike morning on the southwestern edge of the Pacific Ocean. Seymour hunched his shoulders over his laptop in the electronic support section of the main cabin's center section while he accessed his personal e-mail server to look at the details of his college roommate's regrets only dinner invitation to his wedding coming up next weekend. Even though they had meticulously vacuumed their assigned targets, the blunt cut pilot kept their four turbojets on loitering speed at 25,000 feet to give the cryptotechs at the console to Seymour's right and left one last chance to suck up any errant electronic debris from Hainan's Lingshui naval base and pass on to fleet command and submerged offshore submarines through real-time links. In his version of what happened out there and why, Lieutenant Schaefer would explain at the crew's debriefing two weeks later at Hickam AFB, he did not want to land his airborne surveillance platform back at Kadena with a quarter tank of unspent fuel.

Seymour glanced to his left at the other ensign staring at his laptop monitor, and, squinting, he could see groups of numbers. "Hey, you got something good going on there in slow mo, is that a authentic stream of numbers, or do you have a duckie?"

Ensign Ford looked back at Seymour carefully and answered through his very thin lips. "No, we're not going to get anything useful trolling like this. Too close to their lunchtime too, you know. We're done for the day. I'm just looking at the NCAA tournament seeding. I got some big bucks on Michigan State and Duke getting into the final dance."

"Hey, random! Know what you mean. Me too, I'm doing my e-mails. When we're done, suppose we switch back so at least we'll know what our auto storyteller program is sending the WorldWatchers back home, okay?"

Before they could do that, the yellow lights started blinking on their console monitors. "Heads up back there," Lieutenant Schaeffer's voice came over the intercom. "We have visitors, coming up portside. Looks like a couple of Finbacks from Lingshui checking us out. They're late today. But we're okay, 70 miles from their island, on auto and heading zero-seven-zero away from them, real slow."

Even though they have rehearsed this cat-and-mouse game on every one of their VQ-1 ferret flights over Chinese targets before, the crew stopped what they were doing, anticipating the buffeting wake that'll be left by the showoff J-8 pilot flying four times faster at Mach 2 than their EP-3E Aries II. When it happened a few seconds later, it felt like a lullaby lifting them over a low speed bump. But for Seymour, his pulse fluttered when he remembered the det school story of a MiG 21 pilot downing one of these flights a few years back by firing off his PL-2B missiles at the top of a zoom climb. An Air Force interpreter aboard a Sentry radar-in-the-sky flying at 50,000 feet overhead the Chinese pilot yell "Rockets fired! I fixed his ass! I fixed his ass!"

"Hang on gang," Lieutenant Schaeffer interrupted. "It's not over yet. The second pilot's creeping up for a closer look, portside."

Looking out the small portside window, WO4 Allen described what he saw into his shoulder microphone. "Hey, he's getting darn close. Hey, that's too close. He's giving some kind of hand signal. I can see his face. Hey, Ensign Chin," he turned and peered at Seymour behind him at the console. "Hey, even with his flight helmet on he looks like you, sir."

Seymour didn't turn, but flipped Allen a middle finger behind his back. He had never liked him, then or now.

"He's getting too fucking close—I'm going to stay on auto for stability," Lieutenant Schaeffer interrupted again in a tight voice. "Er. Er. Crew, he's taking off under the port wing. We're gonna be dry cleaned. Secure your gear and hang on back there," he instructed.

Seymour and Ford stowed their laptops in the padded velcro harnesses in front of them, and braced themselves by holding onto the console with both hands just as the Finback's roiling exhaust swept over their plane, bumpier this second time.

Then it was Allen on the microphone, "Hey lieutenant, Lieutenant Schaeffer, the first Finback's coming back fast, I can see him sir, portside."

"I see him. What the fuck they doing today? He's right under number one engine."

Before the pilot could finish the next word, a loud, metallic shattering sound reverberated backward through the plane's entire frame, slamming Seymour's head forward into Ford's shoulder, right into his Old Spice® deodorant that Seymour abhorred. Next the Aries' clipped nose lifted up to the right, sending the pair backward away from the console, before the plane veered and dove straight down, gathering speed, its number one engine trashed, its nose clipped, and all five operators in the online electronic support compartment in the main cabin center section tumbling for balance.

"Mayday, Mayday, PB-20N, Kilo Romeo 919, 70 nautical miles SSE of Hainan Island. Mayday. Collision with Finback. 070 at 22,500. Mayday."

Seymour could see by the number 243 on the dock's monitor that Lieutenant Schaeffer had dispatched this repeating distress stream on the international emergency frequency, but nothing came back, no response. From his training Seymour could tell what the lieutenant was thinking and what options existed next—bailing out, ditching in the ocean, or emergency landing.

"Lieutenant Franklin, begin Emergency Destruction Protocols immediately."

"Yes, sir, they're doing it right now, sir, right now," Lieutenant (jg) Franklin, the Annapolis flight officer in charge of mission security repeated, fire ax in hand.

Seymour quickly reached for the frequency keys on the keyboard in from of him and declined every number down to zero; then he quickly ran his batch file and fried it by hitting the dedicated F12 key three times. Lieutenant Franklin walked down the aisle making sure against a master list that every secure radio link was zeroized, then walked back verifying that all classified digital information in the computers had been nuked.

When this part of the checklist had been double-checked, he said to them, "Okay now, your binders, I want all of them," and collected and counted aloud all five—each operational binder printed on acetate-treated paper that will dissolve in water immediately—then dumping them into the two crypto boxes at the end of the aisle.

Next he collected the five laptops, and placing them one at a time on the floor of the cabin, he pulled down the plastic goggles to cover his eyes, the Navy's rare concession to OSHA, and smashed his ax into them, hard enough to make sure that the hard-drives were demolished. Finally, after dumping the two crypto boxes out the starboard over-wing hatch, he confirmed his task to the pilot, "EDP completed, sir."

By now the Aries had leveled out, stabilized at a steady but slower speed.

"Crew, prepare for bail out," Lieutenant Schaeffer's voice came on the com, and Seymour sensed he was agitated. "Chutes, and survival gear," he added.

Seymour reached back across the aisle for his SV-2, helmet, Nomex gloves, and made sure he had the pre-fitted harness chute with his name stitched on it. With his chute still at his feet, he looked at Ford, and then at Allen, each expression betraying the knowledge that since they could bail out only through the portside aft main door, with engine number one out, there was no way the power could be pulled back enough in engine number two to keep them from jumping out and slamming fatally into the Aires tail. Virtual suicide. No option at all.

They also knew that ditching in the ocean was not an option either. As if anticipating the crew's response, Lieutenant Schaeffer said with tight lips, "Condition Five. I'm going in for an emergency landing at Lingshui. They've not responded yet, but I'm going in. This is an emergency. No option. It's their crazy pilot that did this."

Seymour, Ford and Allen floated looks again, surveillance plane, spy plane, ferret flight, violation of Chinese sovereignty, international incident, we're going to be in for it, a nightmare, and Seymour was beginning to ask if he'll leave this island in time for his best friend's wedding in eastern Washington next weekend.

By the time the People's Liberation Army's jeeps and APCs reached the Aries parked at the far end of the main runway, Lieutenant Schaeffer had completed his briefing with the twenty-three crew members cramped into the main cabin. Name, rank and serial number. You can also tell them what happened. Their J-8 pilot rammed and crippled us. He forced this emergency landing. You can tell them that much. (Seymour also knew that since Lingshui housed one of China's most sophisticated electronic signals gathering complexes and upgraded recently, the PLA had witnessed what happened and monitored all their transmissions from the moment the Aries left Kadena.) Nothing else. We're clean on this mission. We have not flown into their air space. Not this time, thought Seymour, halfway between Vietnam and Hong Kong, and within helicopter distance to the contested, oil-rich Parcel and Spratley Islands.

Before Allen opened the main exit door to the cabin, Lieutenant Schaeffer added, "Remember the standing instructions when captured from det school. Anything else is your personal decision, understand?"

When the entire crew had gathered in front of their plane, Lieutenant Franklin jotted down an inventory of the damage: all airspeed sensors gone, large hole in left aileron, nose ring sheared off, elevator bent, HF wire separated and wrapped around tail, engine one's propellers bent where it had cut into the Finback. Built like a tank. Most likely would not have continued to Kadena safely.

The armed PLA had encircled the Aries, and a young and agitated officer approached the crew. "You rammed and killed our fighter pilot. Now you violate China's sovereignty," he yelled and waved through the younger and disheveled interpreter in tow, his tunic unbuttoned and the left epaulet missing, as if he had just grabbed his uniform from the laundry basket.

It was March, but the trade winds from the teaming equator had pushed up this sticky humidity and wrapped itself around Seymour in a fever so teaming thick that he could not clearly distinguish what was happening in front of him from what was being rehearsed or dreamed. In one moment he was standing side by side with his crewmates, but in the next he was standing back several feet away from them and himself as if he were looking at someone else, his double perhaps, a dawdling amateur in a home video.

In one frame he thought he heard Lieutenant Schaeffer insist on talking to the naval base commander, Seymour wasn't sure. But in the video's cut away he could see the PLA officer and interpreter wrestling with the lieutenant in the binary, conventional, male warrior culture of good versus evil, right versus wrong, headman versus headman in a hierarchical deadlock.

"Admiral not here, him in meeting," the disheveled interpreter responded.

The PLA officer-in-charge of the tarmac detail noticed Seymour in the lineup and, pointing his finger straight at Seymour, said something to him in Chinese without his aide's interpretation. Trance or no trance, Seymour could not understand it. On a good day he could say in Chinese "Fuck your mother" and "Wish you a prosperous New Year," but even then he did not know what dialect they were in. So he just stood there quietly mouthing his serial number or Social Security number, he wasn't sure which.

The officer turned and outsourced his accusations to his subordinate for translation. "Spy. Betrayer of mother country. You wear wrong uniform."

"And bad parents, not make you learn mother tongue," the officer added in a sudden surge of English

"You'll not talk directly to my crew," Lieutenant Schaeffer said, stepping between them.

By then the deep green PLA bus had pulled up, and the officer-in-charge ordered his detail to form a V and funnel the Aries crew aboard.

With a final look at the Aries, Lieutenant Schaeffer said, "You leave that plane alone. U.S. property."

For Seymour, standing in that humidity and heat, the entire scenario turned to black and white, and the lieutenant's morphed into Keenan Wynn defending the Coke® machine with his M-1 in *Dr. Strangelove*.

"Grace first," Lieutenant Schaeffer said to the crew standing in front of two long tables for their first meal in the military hotel's cafeteria. "Oh God, our provider and protector, bless our country, family and friends at home. Comfort them in their moment of anxiety. Thanks for bringing our plane and crew down safely. May our stay here be short. And bless the food we are about to eat."

More balanced now in the hotel's air conditioning, Seymour could tell that except for the armed sentries at every exit on every floor, none of the personnel working at the hotel wore uniforms, but by their alertness they were military, even those four bringing bowlfuls of sautéed bok choy, strips of beef with green beans in red bean sauce, braised fish with ginger and garlic, and steaming rice to their tables. At the end of the table Lieutenant Schaeffer picked up the chopsticks in front of him, set them back down and looked up.

But it was Allan who looked at his chopsticks and then at Seymour and said, "Don't know about you, but I never been able to eat with these darn things." Turning to the lieutenant, he asked, "How do we know this food's okay? Maybe they've put some mind-altering drugs in them fish heads or in the mystery meat?"

Seymour thought about suggesting that Allan should be designated the official FT, the Food Tester, and suspected he would prefer fried chicken, Jell-O® and Kool-Aid® at a Mormon picnic, but looked down and kept his mouth shut instead, in this scene he thought he had left behind when he got his diploma and naval gold bars from Wazzu last year. But no, it was reappearing now as something that'd crawled out of a nightmare that would not go away. When the waiters brought the forks to the tables, their heads shaking, Seymour ignored them and picked up his chopsticks. He didn't do it to mollify the PLA officer-in-charge; he did it deliberately just to piss off Allan some more, a gloved challenge to his perception of the world.

Towards the end of the meal, someone at the other table started reciting passages from the New Testament. He rendered parables as if he were stitching together dream fragments into an instructional manual for how they were to behave during their detention on the island. "According to John," he emphasized at the end, "we are the sheep that our Father does not want lost. Believe in him, and he will find us and guide us. Amen."

Seymour kept his head down during this recession, but through his peripheral vision, he thought he saw his roommate Ford look back at him, forehead furrowed. Everyone else kept their heads down, their eyes closed as if in ablution or dream, and their hands folded in prayer in front of them, from the first lieutenant to the last petty officer down the line. Little did the two of them anticipate just how much this initial display of religious fervor will infect their days and nights for the rest of their incarceration on the island.

Within two days, Bible passages were being quoted to each other in the hallways and floor lounges: "Jesus is the truth, Matthew five-two," "Open your heart to the Lord, Luke three-three." They had also started addressing each other as brother or sister. On the third morning, Ford woke up Seymour from a deep sleep.

"Listen, listen to this," he said, shaking Seymour's shoulder to awaken him.

The muffled words "...lightning of His terrible swift sword, His truth is marching on, Glory, glory hallelujah..." drifted into their room, and they could feel the feet above them humping through the ceiling in time.

"Jesus, listen to this," Ford continued. "They can't even get the words to the Battle Hymn right. They're making it up as they go, just like their damn Bible quotations."

"Maybe we should talk to the lieutenant about this, at least not at five in the morning?"

Later, the lieutenant explained it this way. "It'll keep us together, focused as a Christian nation. It'll keep up our morale and spirits. Listen, Allan has a five-dollar pool going. The person who guesses closest to when we'll be released gets to win one-hundred-and-twenty bucks. Not bad, huh? Another morale booster to remind us who we are and what we're doing here.

"You know our president and vice president are not going to forget us. They're both former pilots. They won't let us down; they'll bring us home. These things take time, you know. Politics, uh-huh."

So for the next eight days then, Ford and Seymour felt assaulted and alienated from both sides. For the entire crew and the PLA within hearing distance, The Battle Hymn of the Republic became their daily five o'clock wake up call, Amazing Grace preceded their meals, and the barrage of misquotations from their Bible reverberated throughout their day. Every morning the entire crew was escorted one at a time into the basement laundry area that had been hastily converted into an interrogation room and asked the exact same litany of questions in the same order, the list repeated three times in case of a faulty translation. Apologize or face criminal charges. For ramming F-8 pilot and killing him. For violation of Chinese airspace. For violation of Chinese sovereignty. For Espionage. Apologize. Say you sorry. Accept responsibility. Apologize or face criminal charges, accept responsibility, apologize or face criminal charges, accept responsibility. Until the second week, when the officer-in-charge without the interpreter instructed in English, "Only answer yes, or no, and you can go to your room."

Then over the next week, Seymour followed this sequence of events in the U.S. media's coverage of this international incident. First Newsweek reported that on their tenth day on the island, U.S. Ambassador Joseph Prueher wrote a letter to the Beijing Minister of Foreign Affairs Tang Jiaxuan. In it he expressed President Bush and Secretary of State Powell's sincere regret over this incident, and asked to convey to the Chinese people and specifically to the family of the fighter pilot Wang that they were very sorry for their loss.

On the eleventh day, the entire crew was bused to Hainan's commercial airport where they were charged $34 each for a visa fee before boarding a Continental Boeing 737 loaded with doctors and medical services. At Kadena they were transferred to an Air Force Boeing C-17 Globemaster nicknamed The Spirit of Bob Hope that flew them to Hawaii's Hickam AFB for debriefing and a Job-well-done phone call from President Bush. When Seymour saw the CNN delayed broadcast of their return in his hotel room in Washington while waiting to be escorted to the White House on Pennsylvania Avenue, he looked away from the TV and stared out the balcony at the blue sky over the Mall.

Later Seymour was troubled by the Fox News and *People* magazine coverage of the twenty-four crew members crowded into the Oval Office where they were joined by Vice President Dick Cheney and National Security Advisor Condoleezza Rice beaming at them as returning, bronze helmeted centurions. Hell, he thought, we were just caught and smacked for opening their mail, that's all.

"The vice president and I are thrilled to be able to look you in the eye and say "Thanks for your service to the country,'" President Bush said in his fifteen minutes he spared for the crew.

Still on camera in this photo op, the president shook each one's hand before being photographed with them individually. When he reached Seymour down the line, he squinted at the ensign's name and White House security photo I.D. hanging over his white, dress uniform and turned to look for his prompter as if there had been an error in the prepared script.

*The New York Times* reported next day that Lieutenant Schaeffer had been awarded the Distinguished Flying Cross, the nation's highest military honor, for his airmanship in landing his damaged Aries and crew safely on Hainan Island, and the Meritorious Service Medal for leadership. The Air Medal was given to the rest of the crew. Seymour looked at his medal and wondered what happened to the hotdog pilot who rammed into their Aries.

Back at his home base on Whidbey Island from which he could see Mt. Baker, Mt. Rainier and the Olympics on the ocean side a couple of days later, Seymour found the answer to the follow up on the other side of the Pacific in a copy of Time magazine he had picked up from a convenience store in Oak Harbor. Premier Jiang Zemin had conveyed a decree from Beijing's Central Military Commission praising pilot Wang Wei as a revolutionary martyr, designated him Protector of the Sea and Sky, and called him resolute and daring, cool and calm, heroic and indomitable, who with his life had composed a stirring song of factory for patriotism and revolutionary heroism. After reading this back at the base, Seymour stared at his Air Medal on his dresser for a long time, at the burnished eagle in an attack dive clutching two lightning bolts in its talons overlaid on two, metallic overlapping circular discs hanging from a gold and blue ribboned chevron.

A sidebar featured a story on a joint ventured, entrepreneurial shop named The Apology and Gift Centre with a recent surge in clientele in Tianjin, just a short drive from Beijing. True to its advertising pitch "We Say Sorry for You," it charged clients $5.00 for a surrogate delivery of an apology, and $10.00 for misbehavers who preferred to display their mea culpas on its program "Apologize in Public" that aired on 828 on the AM dial nightly, seven days a week. It also offered a discount for those who wished a lesser and shorter confession of a regrets only message. American Express, Visa, Master Card, Visa and phone cards accepted.

A companion article reported the Chinese refusal to allow the Americans to repair the damaged Aries and fly it out of Hainan. But a compromise was hammered out in Beijing granting the United States permission to fly in a Lockheed Martin's civilian crew to dissemble the surveillance plane and fly it out on July 4 a week later on two leased Russian Antonov-124 cargo planes to its factory in Marietta, Georgia. China also submitted a complaint that the U.S. had flown surveillance planes over Chinese airspace forty-four times since the Korean War, and a bill for one million dollars for the detention and repatriation of the crew, and a two months parking ticket for the Aries, which the House of Representatives voted immediately 424 to 6 against paying.

When Seymour stepped away from the media coverage of this story, he could not be sure which parts actually happened and which dreamed, imagined or exaggerated. He was sorry however he had missed his friend's wedding, and he regretted not winning the $120 evacuation pool, the lieutenant did. Though he did not know exactly why, he was nevertheless determined to make a concerted effort to learn Mandarin, practice to be more agile at using chopsticks, and to request a transfer of his WorldWatcher assignment from VQ-1 to VQ-2 in Spain, so he can better understand his own story.

# FREE KICK

*A girth for pack or saddle; a tight grip;*
*a thing done with ease; a certainty to happen.*
—Webster's for *cinch*

Two years had slipped by since Cinch moved into the interior to be closer to the projects where he did most of his work, but mostly Cinch was here because this was where he wanted to be. While cracking two eggs into the pan over a low propane flame, he counted the number of deliveries he's scheduled to make this morning, five or six. Will there be enough *amoxicillin* much needed by the children this time of year, with or without bubblegum flavoring? He scrunched his eyes, and wondered if such foreign invasion of their immune system is fair trade for the destruction of their traditional diet. Will he be back in time for the meeting with the Minister of Natural Resources and Environment?

It had taken him five months of continuous effort to set her up for this meeting. He never had any doubt about it, though in a challenging moment last month he thought about acquiring a religion for once, just to help it along. But he didn't, and chose instead to focus his energies on getting something done rather than debating over things he could not prove.

He spooned the scrambled eggs onto a porcelain plate and ate standing up. What he could prove was that it could be done. After all, he was used to seeing the seemingly impossible reverse itself in his own country, a country of flimflams and cons in which people willingly believed that dropping an uranium-235 bomb and a plutonium-239 bomb on civilians that indiscriminately killed two-hundred-and-eighty thousand people instantly near half a century ago, actually saved lives. For emphasis, he scrapped a thumbnail across the copper rivets of his porcelain plate. So, in a series of increasingly detailed and provocative letters and e-mails to the Natural Resources and Environment Minister, he added to his daily diet of four hundred lies, on the average. And why not?

Cinch's first letter politely requested a meeting at the Minister's convenience, suggesting that since the two of them had a mutual interest in the continued welfare of the some three-hundred square miles of natural preserve owned by the government—two-hundred thousand acres or roughly half the size of the county in Oregon that Cinch grew up in—they meet to discuss developing some plans for maintaining its ecological integrity. Each subsequent letter and e-mail prompted more discussion items: reforestation and erosion control; protection for the flora and fauna, and of course, including the frogs and cicadas; water conservation and safeguards for water quality; the e-mails in the last month attaching as documents a copy of his graduate degree in forestry, and experience testimonials for fire management and recreation work with the U.S. Forest Service; and the final letter exploring a mutually beneficial program proffering the eleven small villages that ring the lower elevations of this park as a buffer zone against commercial development. Whew! Take that, kiddo. All but where to put the crapper. How can she refuse?

Quatar knocked and came into the kitchen, pouring himself a cup of cold coffee before asking, "Hey, ready?"

Dark-skinned with deep, dark brown eyes suggesting impatience, it was Quatar's final touch in getting a sympathetic friend at the embassy to invite the Minister to a cultural exchange reception two weeks ago where they met at last face-to-face and agreed to this afternoon's meeting. He had also helped Cinch with many of the items on the shopping list sent to M.N.R.E. After all, he had grown up in one of these eleven villages before he went to the city for an education hundreds of miles away on the coast. Now he's back years later, for just about the same reasons that Cinch was here from thousands of miles away.

"Hey, yeah. How many," Cinch started to ask.

Quatar held up the extended fingers of his right hand, a throwback to their early days of working together for a relief organization and fumbling with the language. Cinch knew that Quatar's eyes saw and remembered everything, everything, and suspected that if his friend would one day turn to writing, he would be merciless. "The sixth clinic is closed today. They took someone to the city's hospital last night—not bad, a field cut. The barefoot nurse did her job. We have enough *amoxi* for this morning."

The meeting took place at a former sweatshop the local municipal government in partnership with a civilian action team and the foreign assistance program that Cinch and Quatar worked for took over a couple of years ago. This building had been abandoned two years ago by the garment-manufacturing owners when its workers, women all, unionized and submitted a list of demands to the management. Now, in stepped the Minister of Natural Resources and Environment. Cinch saw her as a quick blonde with double-lined lips, someone misplaced in time and location, or worse. Followed by several aides, she sat uncomfortably on a bench in the former factory that now served as a training center for the villages' barefoot nurses who sometimes also took charge of their domestic violence and children's health care programs.

"You like my rings, no," the Minister asked when she saw Cinch staring at her hands with a ring on every finger, including the thumbs. "Each one is a stone from a different province of the country," she explained.

It dawned on Cinch that while he had some answers, the Minister did not know what the questions were. He looked over at Quatar, who seemed to be fighting sleep or shutting his eyes in impatience. Shrugging his shoulders, he was no help.

"Thank you for coming here," Cinch started saying, first making sure that everyone had a seat and a cold, soft drink in front of them. Having heard about the government's emphasis on its need for transparency, he said, "To be quick, I'm proposing that you transfer the maintenance of this natural preserve to our organization."

Silence, followed by more silence. The Minister was not looking at him.

She sipped on her straw, then said, "You do not have the resources to do it," looking directly at Cinch, emphasizing every word.

"Nor do you," Cinch looked right back at her.

"I have a proposition," he added. "We'll turn this nature preserve into a park with interpretative center, cabins, restaurant and trails. We'll take care of it."

"Wait, wait, wait," interrupted a woman with a baby in the back of the hall. She had stood up and was gesturing with her free hand. "What are we supposed to say to these tourists as we walk them along the trail? Ask them 'Are you enjoying our country today?' We have a shortage of everything. When will we have time to entertain the tourists?" She then asked if anyone's wondered who will clean their toilets and trim their hedges.

Another woman stood up too and said, "We don't have a shortage of nothing."

Several persons laughed, including Quatar, who was avoiding Cinch's searching look on what to say next.

Cinch was facing a dilemma here. Since Shrub had been residing at 1600 Pennsylvania Avenue, his country's compliant news media had served as the middleclass' firewall against radical doubt. And why not? The children of the Baby-Boom generation had swarmed to the schools' communications programs and now as journalists, reporters, columnists, anchors, even boom operators, they're on the job. Their visuals compress time and space, past and present, and with changing images every two seconds and close-ups eliminating cause-and-effect, the viewer will walk away with a dizzying montage of impressions signifying nothing in particular. Yes, yes, change the image, make it up, add more pixels, a lot easier than changing the real thing. Cinch sensed this was the turning moment at the meeting, but he was not exactly prepared for it happening so fast.

"Yes, that's all very true," he looked at the two women in the back of the room. Then he looked straight at Quatar. While he still had doubts if three hundred square miles were sufficient to sustain its biological integrity against encroaching airborne and underground seepage of toxic industrial waste, it was a bit late to back out now. But there's a chance, as there's a mountain range running through the middle of the preserve. "I propose that we play a ninety-minute football game," he said. "Between your Ministry and these villages. The winner will take control of the park."

The Minister looked up, and his assistant leaned over and whispered something to her.

"That's impossible. You can't be serious."

"Yes, I am."

Cinch stood up and added, "Your Ministry doesn't have any funds to do it, the World Bank and I.M.F. want you to privatize it, and in the meantime nothing's being done."

He believed in his convictions, and damn it, he wasn't going to let the strengths of the Peace Corps, World Vision, Mercy Corps, Oxfam, Doctors without Borders or even Opus Dei stop him from doing what needed to be done in wrangling control of this piece of land from the benign government. The villagers will re-learn how to care for it as they've done for centuries, with adjustments for compass and tack, and in return be nourished by it before the Americans seized it and developed it into a destination resort in its harvest of empire.

"This is highly unusual," the Minister said, looking at her assistant. "There is no protocol for this."

Quatar raised a hand and held up five fingers. "A trial period. Let's agree that if we win, we'll have it for a five-year trial period."

The Minister and her assistant looked at the half dozen villagers gathered at the edge of the hall, looking at their shoes, sizing up their chance.

"And what if you lose," she asked, smiling for the only time that afternoon.

Before Cinch or Quatar could say anything, the smarty pants woman in the back yelled out, "We've already lost everything."

But they all knew that they didn't want to lose the same thing twice.

So this was it, this empty schoolyard on Sunday, except for a few neighborhood kids curious about the gathering of fancy vans, pickups and sedans from the city. The Ministry's team of some twenty players had on new Addidas white-and-blue uniforms and matching shoes, accompanied by their own referee with whistle and two linesmen. Cinch knew they're not really the enemy, but they sure look like it with their intimidating warm-up drills. This was only a game, though the stakes were high, at least for us, Cinch thought. On his annual visits with his family in Oregon, Cinch had felt more space slipping in between him and that community in which he spent the first eighteen years of his life, its excesses and self-indulgence displayed for all to see on Friday nights finding its way here on this Sunday.

The Minister walked over to where Cinch was stretching, her hands on her waist, acting astonished, that outraged schoolteacher pose.

"You can't play, you're not eligible, you're not a villager," she challenged.

41

"Why not?" Cinch looked over to the two Peace Corps volunteers dressed in white and blue. "What about them?" In fact he had met one of them before, a gal from Muncie, Indiana, who was a striker on the championship Northwestern team last year. "If they are eligible, so am I." Cinch had always been curious about these Peace Corps volunteers. Here they were, seventy percent of them liberal arts majors. They came loaded with morality but no life skills except for doing e-mails, jogging and soccer. "And besides, we're one player short."

"Okay, okay," the Minister flashed her eyes. "Since this is a friendly game, you can borrow one of ours. We have enough."

Cinch looked over at Quatar, who agreed with him. No way, no defector, turncoat, expat, DP, or worse, a mole, especially on loan. What will be the interest? Who could trust his motive in error or valor?

It was a slow, endurance game. Except for the two Peace Corps volunteers, the first half exhausted every player including the two goalies. The score was tied 0-0 after a penalty free forty-five minutes, as no side could put together a coordinated offense of more than twenty yards or two consecutive passes, whichever was less. Both teams were stretched out on the sidelines drinking water. Cinch and Quatar looked around at their teammates. They wanted to say something encouraging, wave a flag or cheer or something, but they both knew that nothing more was needed to motivate them.

So the second half continued like the first, and several times both goalies left their penalty area to join the offense. Not many players were running anymore. Even when someone had the ball or was marking the person with the ball, it was all in slow motion. Most were visibly panting, hands on waist, and, whenever possible, bent over and sucking air.

Well close to the very last seconds of the game, a short villager with peddling, cucumber legs had managed to dribble the ball all by himself past the last white and blue defender, including the out-of-position goalie who had huffed all his way up to midfield in an all out last minute suicide squeeze. The villager had the ball all to himself and was headed straight for the goal, until the only person still able to catch up with him, that Peace Corps gal from Muncie, Indiana, she made an illegal sliding tackle from the rear in the penalty zone, sending both the ball and player to the side of the goal. Instantly the shrill whistle went up, a penalty kick call with about five seconds left in the game.

The Minister screamed and protested the call, but there was no doubt it was to be a penalty kick.

Who'll take it? Who has a strong and straight kick?

"I'll take it." It was Quatar, and it was the moment he had been waiting for. "Twelve steps out, right? I'll take it."

So it had come down to this. Eighty-nine minutes in which nothing much of anything happened, and now, the whistle, the red card, and a free kick that'll almost always score, in this case, winning the game. Except for Quatar and the goalie, both sides had lined up behind the ball, witnesses to the one-on-one. He moved quickly toward the ball from the right, faked a hard kick that was followed by the diving goalie, and with his left heel behind him, Quatar tapped the ball into the net, a trick shot he had learned in grade school decades ago. That's it. End of game. Wild screaming and cheering. "We got it back" was repeated again and again, at least for the next five years.

# SUBSISTENCE

For my friends
at NFIC in Hayward

*Every damn time I went hunting, I had to kill
something. I don't carry a bow in the woods
any more. I figure you know exactly what I mean.*
—Fred Bear, archer emeritus

H e stepped into Wisconsin's Northwoods in the early morning's disappearing quarter moon, but it was light enough for him to follow his imagined double walking down this exact, same trail fifty feet ahead. This was the way Dixon hunted, using his double's extra eyes to sight well in front of himself instead of just at the ground below him, while reserving his own for accumulating and interpreting the details of what followed each step. What he did not see was that this was to be his last hunting season.

Today he was triple licensed, including tags for deer and bear, and federal stamps for migratory fowl. Yet he carried no weapon, no rifle, shotgun, handgun, or bow, not even a knife. The heavy pack on his shoulders was stuffed with scrapped chicken and pork parts picked up from a Rhinelander butcher, a few tins of Del Monte sardines and opener, a small bottle of anise oil with dropper, a pair of pliers, some baling wire, a few nails, a small hammer, and a pair of leather work gloves.

He could see the dark shape of his duplicate stopping here by a shadowy tree trunk, irritated that his boots were making a scrunching sound with each step on the frost-tipped prairie grass, like the cornflakes he had chewed for breakfast that morning. He didn't want the noise to scare them away. He knew they were still out scrounging for fall's last berries in these early mornings before the sun came up, but he sensed that they were not here this morning, sure because he could not smell them first. At least not at this stand whose bait he's had to restock every weekend in the last two months.

They've been here this past week too. A good sign. The wooden apple crate wired to a white fir's trunk to keep out porcupines, wolverines and badgers had been broken into, there were deep gouge marks on the tree trunk, and all the meat, bones and sardines had disappeared. Dixon could still smell the pungent bear stink wafting from the hair tufts left on the baling wire and crate parts aside from the diminishing sweet flavor of the anise oil. Yes, this could be the guaranteed-shot stand for those two Green Bay optometrists out to bag their first bear on their first hunt ever and ready to pay for it. It'll help with the car and rent payments.

Dixon sat in front of the cabin's picture window smoking a cigarette and looked out at the lake. Not far from shore two men were casting spinning gear from a small, wooden rowboat. He thought they were a little bit late or a little bit early—in season and in time of day—for the fish in this lake, and maybe just a little careless, or brave. They were in the middle of the rifle season, in a game abundant area of the Nicolet National Forest that drew hundreds of recreational deer hunters from Green Bay, Milwaukee, Madison and even as far south as Rockford and Chicago. Every year there were spectacular reports of shooting accidents and their toll on livestock and other hunters. Local dairy farmers either kept their cows in the barn on weekends, or else let them out only in nearby, fenced pastures with the letters C O W painted in international orange on both sides. Knowing that most of these urban hunters did not stray more than a couple of hundred yards from their vehicles, the local hunters who needed the venison for their subsistence found their spots deep in the woods early in the season, safety-pinned plenty of red flagging on their clothing, and avoided using any kind of camo and going outdoors on weekends.

While Bob and Wally were busy getting their new bear rifles ready for the next day over the kitchen table in the next room, Dixon had time to think about what he was doing. His meager salary as a mathematics instructor at the college in Oshkosh was barely enough to cover his phone bill and the occasional novels he read, and his political activism denied him any opportunity for the supplemental summer teaching. To augment his income he first tried bar tending, mostly at night. Subsistence as food, or, one step removed, subsistence as wages. But after mixing cocktails at two respectable lounges in six months—first at a chain motel on the boulevard near the freeway away from town, then three months later at a German-run resort out on the lake—Dixon found he could not tolerate the racist confrontations he faced in every shift, even at the service window. He worried he might just one day cease taking these remarks and questions as jokes and finally leap over the bar in a rage and beat the shit out of the next customer who asked him where he was really from, and if he knew a Benny Wong in San Francisco, in a bar, university, town, county and state that was almost all white, in which Asians in the service sector were acceptable and left alone only in restaurants and laundries, or else expected to be invisible like their other neighbors, the Chippewas, Menominees and Oneidas, except for July Fourth fireworks stands.

For the third fall now, Dixon continued to look out the same window of the same cabin at the same lake, haunted by his own inability to distinguish clearly between subsistence, survival, and necessity. He was growing more uncomfortable that he was here helping others to kill, whether they're doing it to prove their virility as white, male hunters, or because they believed they were protecting their children and women from these marauding bears, that the security of their community depended on these preemptive strikes. Real or imagined, same damn thing. For the moment Dixon remained undecided, determined that he would work it out after this opening weekend.

BANG. A spout of water sprayed the two men in the rowboat out on the lake. A deafening shot from the kitchen. A hole in the picture window glass, the bullet's trajectory just inches from Dixon's ear. The two men threw their fishing gear into the boat and quickly scrambled their oars back to the dock. An accidental discharge while cleaning the rifle, a courier would describe this city slicker news, at the next dinner table, or in another life.

Their drinks appeared to break their tension after their silent drive to Fritz's at yellow-ribboned Long Lake for dinner, one side of the restaurant decorated with a huge Get US out! Of the United Nations sign freshly painted in red, white and blue.

Wally was still shaking his head. "I told him he shouldn't practice loading his rifle inside the cabin," he repeated, taking another sip of his beer. "That was too close," he added, looking at Dixon.

Dixon resisted saying anything. He just wanted this weekend to be over. Instead, he lit another cigarette.

"Okay, okay, I got it. I'll never do it again. Now can we talk about something else, like what're we going to do with the bear after we shoot it at our guaranteed-shot stand?"

"Didn't we decide on the way up that we'll donate it to Fuzzy Thurston's Left Guard Restaurant, you know, for his bear stew free off the menu on the weekend of the annual Bears-Packers game?"

Dixon looked at the lights of a few houses on the lakeshore in the lingering sunset. He was sure Bob and Wally were not prepared for this endgame of their hunting story—what were they going to do with it after it's shot, killed, a two-hundred-and-fifty pound carcass.

"You have a good sausage recipe and butcher who'll process some of it for yourself," he asked, sure that they didn't. He's been here before. "Or a Mormon taxidermist who'll make you a rug out of the hide?"

The no-problem waitress interrupted them with their entrees, turf and surf for all three, including steak sauce.

"Tell me, Dixon, how did you get into this? All we know is that you're a teacher in Oshkosh, and we've seen pictures of you a couple of times in the *Milwaukee Journal* in some protest march."

Uncertain how things might go otherwise, he decided to answer Bob's question. He'd cashed in on years of hunting in Idaho, and his extensive map reading and aerial photo interpretation work with the U.S. Forest Service in Montana. Most of it was true, but Dixon embellished it here and there out of mischief or boredom at its annual repetition. That's why he was reading fewer and fewer novels, convinced that they contained nothing more than disguised conversations between imbeciles. He could not even trust that Canadian writer, who'd written, "If you build it, they will come," as if he were describing the carefully selected and baited stands he had worked on all summer.

"Why do men hunt?" Wally asked next. "I mean, it's not all that challenging is it, getting a deer, or a bear."

"Yes," Bob joined in. "Wouldn't it be more of a challenge hunting each other, like what's his name, Ice T in *Surviving the Game*?"

The ever-polite guide now, Dixon decided to follow the scripted safari dinner conversation. "You might switch from the unarmed unnatural enemy and go after someone who's locked and loaded with an AK47 or M16 and wearing body armor and can shoot back? Sure, why not, we're the only species on earth that kill each other."

"You've said this before, Dixon, but I want to ask it again. Are you sure these black bears are not dangerous," Bob asked, looking for the waitress to order another drink.

He watched as his double took over this answer. "Absolutely. They'll run from you before you have a chance to sneeze. And besides," he added, setting his knife down for emphasis, "you'll smell it long before it can see you. The only thing you'll have to worry about here are other hunters, poison ivy, ticks and mosquitoes, and it's too late for them."

He sat on a stump in the gloaming smoking another cigarette. Not wanting to be next to their trigger itch, he'd left Bob and Wally at the stand a half-mile away about an hour ago. "Just be quiet and don't move. Be patient—it might take two or three hours. Keep your eyes open, and most of all, keep the barrels of your rifles away from each other," he cautioned, as he walked away downwind from them.

Thinking that he smelled something, he quietly put his cigarette out in the loam beneath his boots and waited, looking in the direction of the stand. Even when he heard the distant bang of a rifle shot from that direction, he continued to sit still. He knew it was from Bob's Weatherby overkill .340 magnum. He could not forget it from yesterday, that explosion still reverberating in his inner ear, the same sound that now echoed back from the eastern escarpments. He could see the 250 grain semi-pointed expanding bullet hurtling through the air and entering the bear just below the neck, clipping a lung and ripping apart a kidney before leaving a huge, bleeding hole at its left flank. Dixon could hear no second shot. Then he looked at his watch, and counted an eight-minute walk back to the stand. Time enough.

When he got there, Bob was hysterical and kneeling next to the downed bear, his Weatherby in one hand, and gesturing wildly with the other. Wally was standing to the side, fumbling with his digital camera. They were both speechless, but kept on pointing to the bear, finally one of them yelling, "The bear, the bear," but Dixon was not sure who.

"A good shot, maybe thirty yards." Dixon shouted back. "You checked if it's dead yet?"

When he walked over to their side of the stand, he could see the bear lying in the dust on its stomach, still sucking air through its flared nostrils, a dim fire left in her eyes. He quickly drew his .357 sidearm, pointed its barrel behind the bear's visible ear, and pulled the trigger, thinking that he had just participated as a good soldier in this scene of ecological imperialism, in which a life was taken needlessly and the environment destroyed in order to make up his professor's deficient salary, oh, such an imagined Eden.

When Dixon got out of his pickup to go to the stand and collect the leftover trash the next morning, he was troubled by the distant, unmistakable high-pitched racing roar from four Kawasaki 650 ATVs' twinned engines. He shouldered an empty pack and his loaded Winchester .270.

By the time he reached the edge of the managed clearcut near the stand, the Kawasakis had caught up with him. When he heard the engines shut down not more than fifty steps behind him, he sensed trouble. Turning around slowly, he could see four men in full camos and face paint swagger towards him with their rifles.

"Hey buddy," the man with black camo face paint called out. "What are you doing out here?"

"Yeah, man," the shortest one with green face paint repeated, un-gloving his right hand and moving its fingers to the trigger guard. "What're you doing here?"

Dixon looked from one to the other and answered. "Same as you, hunting."

"Yeah," the first one challenged, "but you're on private land."

"Didn't you see the posted signs all around," the short one added.

Dixon pretended to look to his left and to his right. "There're no signs here, and I know this is the Nicolet National Forest—that's not private, it's public."

"Yeah, but it's private to you, chink," the first one said.

"You don't belong here, and you can't hunt on our land."

"I pay my taxes, same as you, even when I don't think I should," Dixon told them, certain that this conversation was going nowhere, before turning away from them.

He started counting when he started to slowly walk away from them.

By the sixth step of this nightmare, his double in front of him heard a loud explosion behind him and felt a bullet whistling past both of them, breaking a tree limb and slamming into its trunk less than a foot away. Dixon stood aside and watched his double quickly wheel around, unshouldering his rifle, the safety already off, on one knee, his index finger pulling the trigger and flipping the bolt handle back up with the open palm in one crisp motion, his thumb then pushing the bolt forward and locking it in one stroke and pulling the trigger again, repeating it and then again, all before anyone could take another breath.

Dixon walked over to the four bodies sprawled beside the trail, his heart pounding inside and his head shackled by despair. He knew in a few moments he would be cuffed and asked to repeat this impossible story word by word. For now, all he could see were the letters crawling across their faces beneath the paint.

# CHINK FOOD

Winter's freezing temperatures arrived early this Thanksgiving week, and two local deerslayers still in their wet and muddied camos got out of their pickup parked downtown and waited for passersby to stop and admire their four-point carcass laying in the back, its head propped over the side, two drops of blood congealed just below its flared nostrils. Disappointed no one stopped in awe or shock at their kill, the two hunters entered the Golden Dragon for an early lunch. Here in eastern Oregon it was not unusual for hunters to parade their recent kills down Main Street, a legacy born since subsistence hunting disappeared more than a century ago, along with the bow and arrow, and at about the time the restaurant's current owner's grandfather was allowed out of San Francisco's immigration processing station, *Angel Island*, after a ten-month detention. He had skipped over California's panned out gold gulch in order to fulfill his childhood dream of sailing east to come to the west, and now these two hunters were entering his grandson's restaurant at the end of the parade instead of following the scripted tradition that scooted these hunters to some tavern at the edge of town for the rest of the day.

Inside the restaurant Wing Fee stroked his white goatee that reached down to the top of his tee shirt and asked if his son would wait on them. "Here's the lunch menus, and the specials," he added, and walked away.

"Sure. I drove three hundred miles up the river to come home for the holidays just to wait on these two great white hunters!" Moon fumbled with the place settings, deciding on the chopsticks, and then asked, "Do I call them *kimasabe*, and teach them how to field dress their deer too, that's just sitting out there and beginning to deteriorate, even in this temperature?"

The two hunters walked into the Golden Dragon, nodded a curt acknowledgement to their former teammate Moon, slid into a naugahyde booth opposite each other, shoved aside the chopsticks, took the menus and ignored his suggestion about the lunch specials.

"Just bring us some beer," said the hunter with the black onyx high school graduation ring and a *Smoke a Camel* over a riflescope's crosshairs hat without looking up.

"Yah, and leave the pitcher," his friend added, looking at the menu and moving his index finger down the page very slowly.

Past the swinging doors and back into the kitchen, Moon rolled his eyes at his father and started tapping the beer. "You know, Dad, I didn't think much of it when I went to school with these guys for twelve years, played on the same teams, even Legion ball in the summers, and watched the same movies. Now they don't recognize me anymore, or pretend not to."

Wing Fee nodded and continued dicing the onions and then the celery.

"But each time I've come home in the last four years," Moon continued, "each time it got to be harder understanding how I did it, you know, with these guys walking around like they hated and owned everything? The last couple of times I almost turned around at Hermiston until I decided I wasn't going to let these bozos drive me out of my home when we've been here a couple of generations longer than they have."

Moon's father stopped his dicing, and waved the cleaver at him. "You think these guys give a shit about your history lessons? They have a right to what they believe. At least they're not calling you *Celestial* or *Heathen Chinee* anymore."

"Not to our face anyway. Besides, what's the difference? Around here we're still doing the same thing we've done for more than a century: domestics, washing and ironing their clothes, cooking their food and looking after their gardens. Whatever happened to white arsenic powder that can easily masquerade as monosodium glutamate?"

"Hey back there, where's our beer," one of the hunters yelled, his voice cackling with hubris and rage.

"See what I mean, Dad. How did you do it, all these years?"

Moon met his friend at the casino's café. Junior had been discharged from the Army only days before the U.S. invasion of Afghanistan.

"That was close, even stationed in Germany."

Moon looked him over and smiled. They had been a great double play combination in high school and Legion ball, even when Junior was too tall and too bow-legged for a second baseman.

"You look the same, except for your hair. What was it like, in Frankfurt for two years?"

"It was okay. The Army's the Army, no surprises. At the beginning I traveled around a bit, until I ran into all these Germans who thought they were more Indian than me. Man, one of them actually gave me a lecture on the histories of the Yakamas, Umatillas and Cayuses while his drunken friend kept on calling *Manitou*. Then there's this. This sexy blonde in Hamburg who looked like she could have been the founder of the Black September Movement, she accused me of being a traitor to my people by enlisting in Army, until I reminded her that this is my country first."

They started walking the floor in the direction of the gaming tables, stopping to greet old friends.

"Hey Junior, I heard you're back. What happened to your hair," asked a woman who looked as if she had just stepped off the set of a television serial. "Did the Germans scalp you?"

Junior bent down and gave her a hug, "No, no, no, Marilyn. It was the French that were into scalping. But then you've always had things backwards. Does your car have a forward gear now?"

The croupier at the roulette wheel nodded at them before waving off all bets.

"Junior, Junior," Moon urged. "Go for it, Junior, go for Seventeen. It's going to be Black Seventeen."

Moon knew that Junior did not believe in the casino, even if it kept Tamastslikt and Crow's Shadow going. A white man's tax, Moon had argued.

"Yes, you can call it that, but it's the wrong white man that's getting taxed," Junior had said years ago. "Have you seen the fastest growing industry in Pendleton since this casino opened? Payday loan companies. People are pawning their pickups, trailer homes, RVs, jetboats, maybe things they shouldn't have in the first place, but they're losing them."

"You mean don't exploit people's weakness for a fast buck? You forget that's how they won the west in the first place."

They both watched as the ball clicked to a stop and landed on Red Five, adjacent to Black Seventeen.

"Hey Moon, you can't even get the right color. You learned that over in Corvallis?"

"It's worse," Moon said, hoping there would be this chance to talk to his friend about it. "Red is Green, and Five is Seventeen. Doesn't matter what's real, only what's perceived to be real. That's about it. Last year now, majoring in communications, and I've been looking at jobs. Public relations or advertising. Same thing. What I've learned is how to tell the best lie as often as four hundred times a day."

Junior knew Moon did not want to take over the Golden Dragon either. But their options were limited, without leaving this, their home, where they trusted the daily collusions of sky and firmament. They knew the locations and shapes of things, and what inspired confluence and bottomweed beyond the circumference of the next ridge. Over the years they had even learned tolerance in this sacrifice zone of corporate and military fallout. But this tolerance did not extend to these new arrivals with their yellow ribbons and *Save Our Dams* bumper stickers. Junior and Moon were not about to leave and surrender their home to them, even when Wing Fee hung the American flag in front of his restaurant.

"Hang out and wait and see," Junior answered. "Maybe take a couple of writing courses over at LaGrande. Maybe go into business with you. Let's go see what your father has to say about all this, no?"

"Ah, my other son, you're back. It makes me very happy to see they let you out of the reservation, Junior."

"And yes, Old Man, and I see they've let you come above ground.'

Moon was used to their greetings, a reference to his great grand father's arrival in Pendleton when the Chinese were forced to either live and love in someone's garden shed or in the underground tunnel community beneath the town, or else tied to a horse and dragged out of the county.

"You've been gone three, four years. You must be hungry," Wing Fee beamed. "Here, sit down, let me fix you up some Chinese snacks."

"Great. As long as we don't sit in the same booth that those hunters sat in this morning—bad karma. Moon told me about their twenty-five cent tip too."

Into the kitchen then, he quickly mixed together some tiger prawns with shallots, sugar, salt and pepper before blending them in his electric *Mixmaster*, adding egg white at the last minute. Then he rolled small pieces onto a piece of sugar cane, and finally grilling it for a few moments before serving it on a bed of hot vermicelli, chopped herbs from his garden in the back, and butter lettuce dipped in fish sauce.

"Here, authentic Chinese food, maybe from the south." He had brought the plate to the booth where Moon and Junior were in deep discussion about their business venture. "This is not deep fried heart attack fast food. There's no soy sauce, oil, or MSG. And there's not a lot. Definitely not chink food. And beer does not go with it. Maybe sake, but you didn't hear that from me."

Junior picked up the chopsticks and rolled his eyes. "Here, sit down and eat with us. You've been standing up and serving for more than a century."

"So, Dad, this is definitely great. And it's south all right, really south, like Vietnam? Why don't you change your menu and begin to serve up some real Chinese dishes? Compete with Raphael's down the street? Dim sum at lunch, lighter fare?"

Wing Fee and Junior looked at each other, waiting for the other to say something.

Finally his father smiled and said, "Moon, my son, you're Chinese—you wouldn't understand."

"Okay, Moon," Junior started. "You know there're only two other chink restaurants left in this town, in this *western* town. After the Engs moved theirs up the hill away from the new Harley-Davidson store and upscaled their menu to pan-Asian, by Round-Up time three months later they were whispering Chapter Eleven."

"Yeah, and you just don't move the location of a restaurant in a town like this. And besides, Moon, my son, they don't really like chink food, with the same dark sauce and same light sauce spread over the alleged Mongolian beef or Szechuan chicken and anything and everything else dark or light, as long as they have beer to wash it down with. They just want us to continue cooking for them."

Moon's father walked back into the kitchen and returned with a handful of fortune cookies. "Here, he said, I made the fortunes myself," he said.

Junior opened one and read it. *Don't leave any chance behind.*

"What's this, Old Man?"

Moon's said *Beware of compassionate conservatives.*

"Hey Dad, what are these?"

But by then Wing Fee was already back in the kitchen, taking a step towards the cutting block and very carefully, reached for the dicing cleaver, laughing himself into the new century, and smiling that his family was enjoying the food he had put together for them.

# THE LUNCH

*Take that, Amy Tan*

Two half-sisters walked into a bar in the California that is Chinatown. Since they didn't like each other in the half-English and half-Cantonese of their mother tongue, they sat at separate tables but within sight, text-messaging digital English right into their cell phones. After her drink arrived, the older one keyed a message—YOU GO PICK UP LO MO!—and poked the Send keypad with a lacquered fingernail, sucking on an ice cube and waited for the reply.

WHY?

SO SHE WON'T PLAY THE SPANISH LOTTERY ANYMORE, STUPID, she poked again, but there was no exclamation point this time.

NO-NO, WHY ME PICK HER UP, YOU STUPID. YOU DRIVE FANCY VOLVO.

Treason, she slurped through the ice and looked up at her slightly shorter half-sister seated at a table no more than twenty feet away, one hand over electric lipstick, giggling and finger-wagging a caution this time. Treason, she repeated, loud enough for the bartender to turn her head.

You two ladies okay? she waved a dirty bar rag at them.

They both turned and fixed her with a mind-your-own-business or shut-up stare, whichever worked, before the one with the lipstick collected all her stuff and recollected herself at the other's table—after all, like her or not, she had a rep to keep in this community, since she owned her own consulting business, Efficiency Solutions, providing fuction:time-effort-wage analysis at a hefty fee.

All right, all right Ida, she said and slid her military spec compliant cell phone into her handbag. We got to get Lo Mo out of her condo to talk to her about this lottery together. Lunch or something. Just a suggestion, she shrugged and looked away.

You're right, Ida chunked an ice cube back into her drink and continued. She called me this morning and wanted more money. Invest in my business, she said. It's her business now, she said, Nerissa's business. One hundred bucks for Western Union money transfer, must be wired today, she insisted, to protect her number's eligibility. In the four years she's been playing Spanish Lottery she has lost all her savings, and the monthly interest alone on her credit card loans is staggering and beyond her pension payments.

Or pay her phone and electricity bills for the last two months, Buddhist, Catholic, woodcutter or Kafka, same thing, you know.

What's that? Ida squinted.

That's an expression my anthropologist friend is always using, you know, the one who names everything she has Kafka, even her black lab and her laptop, the one who's licensed by the state to evaluate a person's cognitive condition. We can give her the money for her lottery, or pay her bills, what's the difference, same thing. At least this way she'll have heat and a phone, she added this last part in her falsetto street Cantonese.

But she'll call us ten times a day on it, ten progenitor lectures a day.

Let her phone bill lapse, is that what you're suggesting, sister Ida?

Why, sister Kate Blue, you are so mean!

They had landed on the Dragon 2000 for lunch because they knew it was Nerissa's favorite restaurant in town, even when they've never been there and, not wanting to pick her up from her condo, both pretended not to know where it was, when they had both MapQuested its location at the Palm Court Shopping Center just in case. Shanghai cuisine, you know, where she's from. Exiled sixty-plus years back to the end of the War of Resistance last time, time of her country's last political revolution, Mao's revolution and civil war, one of the half-sisters said. She can remember the food, the dialect and the humidity that much, imagine that, even after a forty-year layover south in Hong Kong where she found a medical career and learned to cuss equally dirty in both privileged and street Cantonese.

Kate Blue had decided it'd be best if Ida would drive her stepmother in her Volvo, as she had to pick up some important papers at the state courthouse. You know, she convinced her, the conservatorship form. Just to irritate her, Ida asked the bartender for a phone book and pretended to flip through the Yellow Pages for the street address of the Dragon 2K. Where is Botelho Drive? she finally looked up and smiled.

Before Ida had time to set the handbrake on the car in the restaurant's parking lot, Nerissa asked her for a hundred dollars. When her stepdaughter peered over her driving glasses at her, she explained, With your sister's friend for guest, it's Chinese manners that the family elder picks up the check.

Not wanting to say there was no such Chinese thing, thereby challenging her stepmother, and suspicious but not knowing exactly why, Ida counted out five sequential Andrew Jacksons from her wallet and handed them to her

And where is your sister? Nerissa demanded. She is late.

But she wasn't, she was opening the door and reaching for her mother's walking cane and helping her out.

Where is your friend? She is late, Nerissa repeated.

Hello Ma. Good to see you too.

Don't be so sarcastic. And keep your eyes on the ground and not at your half-sister. I don't want to fall down and break my fragile ninety-year old hip.

Ma, you're not ninety.

But I will be, tomorrow, she said and tapped a lamppost this time with the black rubber tip of her cane for emphasis, a practiced artifact.

The anthropologist friend was waiting for them by the fountain inside the courtyard entrance to the restaurant.

Nerissa, my mother, Kate Blue looked at her and began the introduction. This is my friend.

Not Nerissa, she interrupted. It is Doctor Zhin.

But Ma, you haven't practiced medicine for more than forty years. The last twenty years of your career you were a hospital administrator, remember? Blowing her loose bangs in her friend's direction, Kate blue added, with her Ph. D. Kelly here is more a doctor than you.

I am very honored to finally meet you, Doctor Zhin, Kelly leaned down and extended a hand, smiling. I am Kelly Hwang. Over the years I have heard so many good things about you.

Yes, yes. So tall. You Korean? And how did you two meet?

Ma, Ma. You know that already. We were classmates at Pembroke, you remember, and my other best friend Suzy Weaver who later changed her name to Sigourney, a.k.a. Lieutenant Ripley. You came to our commencement in Providence, but everything was so chaotic that weekend nobody got to meet anyone, you know.

Nerissa stared at her daughter, distracted momentarily. Sure, sure, she recovered quickly. I mean how did the two of you meet here in California? Waving her cane away from the Pacific Ocean, she smiled and announced with authority, Rhode Island is at the opposite side of this continent.

You know, she peppered a mimicked addition.

They took turns reading the menu aloud. Soup dumplings dipped in black vinegar and ginger sauce, definitely, xiao lung bao. Pink crab dumplings. Rice wine-marinated chicken. Braised sliced beef. Shanghai noodles. Meatballs draped in cabbage, so finely textured they are part pâté, part soufflé. Vegetarian duck too.

What's that? Kelly asked.

That's thin sheets of braised tofu folded over mushrooms to look like duck, Nerissa lectured to everyone at the table, including the waiter. Those vegetarian Buddhist monks have this long tradition of making tofu taste like anything you want, on the hoof or in the air. Besides meditating and sweeping the steps, what do you think they do all those days and nights in those stupas? But be careful, this Shanghai cooking is complex and rich, not like the Cantonese. My favorite is the smoked pork and the smoked fish, big chunks of it, sweet and flavored with anise.

No, not that, not the smoked fish and the smoked pork, Ida said to the waiter. Too much fat and too much salt. Not good for your heart and your arteries.

What are you now, a dietician? Nerissa vexed astonishment. Look at you, you should talk. You're too thin, like you have TB or AIDS. Don't you think I know what's good for me? I've been my own physician since your father left us thirty-seven years ago; I can take care of myself. You, she pointed at the waiter suddenly, surprising him in Shanghai dialect. You bring the smoked pork and the smoked fish and leave the check with me.

Nerissa placed her Visa card on top of the check later, and told Kelly that she felt very lucky that day. My lottery number has been pre-selected to win, and the money is coming any moment, any moment now. It's been my business: I'm taking care of its initial investment, the federal and state taxes, and its eventual profit distribution. Just look, look at these numbers on my fortune, 5.8.5189.

When the two half-sisters saw the annulled platinum Washington Mutual credit card, they looked at each other and went to work at once: they hadn't had a Shanghai mother-and-stepmother for a combined one-hundred-plus years for nothing. While Ida talked about the sudden fortune and eternal prosperity associated with these numbers, Kate Blue muttered something about having to get back to work, and it'll be faster if she took the check and Lo Mo's credit card to the front counter rather than wait for the waiter to come back. On the way there she got out her own credit card, and made a fancy explanation to the manager picking his teeth with a toothpick at the cash register.


What do you think? The two half-sisters asked at the same time the next day they met with Kelly at the same bar.

Well, I can tell you one thing for sure. She's a survivor. And she's mean as hell to you two, and it's not from Alzheimer's. She's driving you two crazy and making you bleed. Wow, one nasty lady who is used to wielding abusive power, especially over you, Kate Blue, my friend.

Yeah, yeah, I knew that, she said between sips, losing the shine of her electric lipstick on her glass. Her political idols are G. Gordon Liddy and Newt Gingrich—power personalities. Even has autographed photos of them in her bathroom.

But what about the conservatorship, Ida asked. Can it be done?

Ida, I'm on your side, to keep California's Adult Protective Services out if for no other reason, Buddhist, Catholic, woodcutter or Kafka. Once they're in, it's almost impossible to do anything else. But I don't know. Just because she believes in this game of chance, a one in three-hundred-and-thirty million, it is still a chance, still a possibility. Maybe that's not enough.

What! But she's not paying any of her bills, the utilities, phone, condo dues, credit card interest, we are. She's not capable of managing her affairs.

I disagree. Not managing her affairs does not necessarily mean she's incapable of doing it. You're doing it for her. She's sharpened her wits enough to get you two to do it for her. She's managing you. Her business now means she has something to do in her retirement. I saw the credit card switch, so did she, and pretended not to.

Ida and Kate Blue stared silently at each other and ordered another drink.

What about addiction disorder? one of them asked.

Nope. No California court is going to accept that one.

What about mild dementia or mild schizophrenia? asked the other.

The court will go buzzing with that, but such an alternate personality substitution is very challengeable. Doctor Zhin can do that herself, without the help of an attorney.

Then they discussed other possibilities—diminished capacity, cognitive dysfunction, emotional impairment, delusional thinking, and ability to remember past presidents—but it was clear to them that Nerissa could clear all these tests. None even looked promising enough to pursue, not even the thought of hiring a religious healing practitioner allowed by the State of California.

After Kelly left, the two half-sisters continued talking like this, past the bar's closing hour and well into an imagined past perfect tense with their mother-and-stepmother and how their family had been fractured and then collapsed back in their country's past century's accumulated wars, revolutions and chance.

# THE ROCKETS' RED GLARE

**M**oon. Moon. Moon Fee, wake up your dad, he tossed his braids back and yelled upstairs. There're ten angry Indians out there whapping the door to get in. Turning the hidden key to the back door, Junior slipped into the Golden Dragon, as if he had spent half his life in this restaurant. Get him to fire up the wok, he added.

Bet they're big and starving too, Moon shook himself down the stairs, astonished at seeing his reflection in a coat-and-tie in the landing's mirror.

Hungry enough to blow down the door for your star-spangled buffet.

Sure, sure. That's only because no one else would serve you people in this county, or even let you stay in town after sundown, except in prison.

They knew this was true enough even when they were in grade school, about the time they squealed and nicknamed the lunch buffet commodity chink food—like Indian fry bread—with chicken parts and veggies thrown in and awash in oil, garlic and soy sauce. Here in RV land this side of the Pacific, the only thing Chinese about this food was the cook. Great for loggers and miners a century ago; great for diabetes and heart attacks today.

Dad's got most of the food out already, Moon poked the trays and lit the alcohol burners under them.

He's lightened up on the garlic in the green beans today. My favorite, always, with its tangy after taste. Junior lifted his nose when Moon got closer. Hope you change your deodorant before the prison interview, or they just might give you the twenty-four hour job instead of the eight.

It's not prison, Moon slapped past him. It's the correctional institute, the largest employer in town, he continued, not looking at him, even bigger than your damn casino. And besides, it's the media liaison position, nothing to do with inmates.

Sure, and that's what your communications degree prepared you for, right? To make sure those who hold the tear gas canisters communicate with those in the orange jumpsuits, right?

How quickly they'd slipped into this argument, a habit from years of balancing each other out, wanted or not. Out in the main dining room Moon's father Wing had made sure the tables were cleaned and set, that there was enough ice and water and checks and toothpicks and fortune cookies ready and chopsticks just-in-case.

All right, all right, he said, sucking on an ice cube. Twenty years I've been listening to you two. I can tell from your arguing someone has done something wrong. He looked at Junior, then at his son before flipping the light switch behind him. I still can't tell, he squinted. Who is it? he finally asked, ignoring the banging on the front door.

They were both looking at Moon, but Junior found the words. He's dressed up for the job interview. Coat-and-tie, it's not like him. Better get out the camera for this special occasion. Jumbo prints. Not since last Thanksgiving.

We're not going to talk about that Junior, remember? Wing reminded him. But it was too late. More banging. They burst into laughter at last Thanksgiving's disaster when Moon brought home his Mormon girlfriend from California, another com major whose role model was Connie Chung, explaining later that maybe it was because her father was from Taiwan, and maybe that too was why everything about eastern Oregon irritated her so much, especially its sloughing ponderosas and Douglas firs.

Wing wanted to say something more, but it was too late. Moon was already out the door with his car keys. The extravagance of the joke will just have to wait, a memory retold so it won't be forgotten.

Moon didn't like this guy who interviewed him at the prison, even from the beginning of the application process when cursory e-mails were their only contact. Illiterate, with bursts of bureaucratic deceit. Moon had suspected a bad liar. Face-to-face there he was—from Human Resources and certified by both the feds and the state, according to the framed testimonies in his small office—and it was worse. Now a third parchment certified he had a com degree from the same state university on the west side, just like Moon's, a double indemnity now. And maybe it was because he could not stand the flecks of broccoli caught in this bumpy guy's upper front teeth. Hey, it was right after lunch, Moon thought and gave him another chance, until he started talking about the Beavers' football prospects next season, putting him just one lie away from wearing the prison-issued blues.

Then there're a few questions here for you, the man started into the interview, the same for all the candidates. But under no circumstance must the questions and answers include any reference to gender, age, nation-of-origin, religion, marital status or race, he added.

Sure enough, Moon thought, no illegal discrimination on these five items here in this land of the free and home of the brave. Except say, can you see answers to four of them, gender, age, nation-of-origin, and race right in front of your eyes, can't you? Or say, Junior was always asking when he's had enough whiskey or beer or both why there're more Indians inside the prison than outside, and then there are those times when there's not enough of either. Don't mention race, not in the Q&A and not in the FAQ, and definitely not here in eastern Oregon's twilight's last gleaming.

Moon's great, great grandfather had sailed east to get to the west, and now more than a century later Moon's flying west to get to the east at night on a Boeing 747 from SFO. Since he walked out of the prison interview a month ago—leaving Mr. Human Resources astonished and spluttering—Moon and Junior had decided to go into business as partners. Open up a fireworks stand. The true red-white-and-blue Americans' fixation to celebrate their nation's birthday in the middle of their perpetual war on terrorism hired pyrotechs to transport these patriots into awestricken eyewitnesses and torch the fuse for the next quixotic revolution. From a fire crackhead family, Junior had the legal sovereignty permits. But now as Moon fidgeted with the lint on his jacket's Velcro strip and looked past Junior out the port window at the massive Pratt and Whitney engines' thin blue exhaust, he's not so sure. Fireworks are cheaper in China than South Dakota. We invented it. Better profit, Wing had said, trust me, I still have relatives there.

Moon was skeptical when his father made the phone calls and set up a meeting with a very distant relative he had never met—a fourth cousin on his great, great grandmother's side, a Chuck Mok—just as he was equally uncomfortable about how he might be treated, looking like a Chinese but not knowing a single word of the language, except what he had learned at a bar from a Hong Kong exchange student at college one night, maybe a passable *Due-nay-low-moe—Fuck your mother*—in Cantonese, which he knew enough was not even in the national dialect, at least not for more than the last half century since 1949.

In the last half century Chuck Mok has done well, especially since 9-11, made millions. You see, he explained with his fork at Kowloon Hotel's extravagant lunch buffet of buffets he was hosting for Moon and Junior, the factory I owned made American broad stripes and bright stars in all shapes and sizes: flags, sweaters, hankies, ties, socks and stockings, decals, bras and shawls, even doormats. For two years there was so much business I had to double the workforce in Shenzhen every month to make sure the flag was still there. I made so much money I had to sell the fucking business in Shenzhen and retire south to Hong Kong.

You mean your factory was already making these flags?

No, of course not. But when I saw your network news announcer describe the bomb explosions over Baghdad as beautiful 4th of July birthday celebrations, I knew your country would have a post-9/11 rush to patriotism. My only decision was which was easier, to modify the factory for the flag or the magnetic Support-the-War –the-President –the-Troops Freedom-Is-Not-Free stripes for cars and trucks and lapel buttons. So now, distant cousin's son, how's your Chinese?

*Nee how?*

What's that?

*Nee how mah?*

Sounds like a squeaking French frog with a Shanghai accent. What is it?

It's how are you? Moon interpreted himself. What're you, a fucking linguist?

Wing Fee said you're not really retired, Junior saved him. No one in Hong Kong is ever retired, he said.

I make introductions. I connect the dots—I connect people with the same interests and needs. A Hong Kong specialization, you know, a service. In the long run, it pays off for everybody. And you, besides running a fireworks business? Who are you?

A Umatilla. Went to school with Moon here, who was struggling with his chopsticks when his father taught me how to use the wok. When he went to college, I was in Afghanistan training its national army in intelligence work. You know, where to look for smoke signals and how to read them. It was pretty stupid, since they've lived there for hundreds of years and sure as hell knew more than we did. I like cooking better.

You're different, Chuck Mok pointed with his fork again. I met another Indian once; he was different too. I think a French Fence-post from Canada, on his way to an audience with Queen Elizabeth in Buckingham Palace I think. This guy stopped by here for some fireworks too. A long way, he said, reversing the Columbus voyage, he said, going west to get to the east, or did he say going east to get to the west, you know? And then he lowered his head and muttered something about a gunpowder plot to blow up someone's house.

Then, looking to Moon, I can see why you two are friends, he added.

Chuck Mok did indeed take care of everything at the fireworks factory at his hometown just two hundred yards north of Hong Kong over the ramparts and past the double checkpoint Charlies and puff, there it was, Shenzhen and mainland China. Everything. Wing Fee was right and gave proof—because Mok was a relative, everything was discounted, including the priority shipping and customs-clearing documents for San Francisco. Extravagant bursts. Vibrant crackles. Hanging gold willows. Chrysanthemum whistles. Parachute fountains. And a 72-shot Armagedon Brocade Finale bursting in air. All this under Junior's certified enrollment number.

When they were back at the hotel lobby, Chuck Mok opened his cell phone to a call from Oregon. For Moon, he closed the phone and put it back in his pants pocket. There is no other way to say this. Go home now. Wing Fee has passed away. Last night. Massive stroke. I'm very sorry.

Both Moon and Junior were struck down in their surprise and sorrow. The flag lowered from Mt. Suribachi. A father to them both. Together they remembered listening to him a few years back drinking a cup of chrysanthemum tea in his orange formica kitchen next to a life-size cardboard cutout of John Wayne from The Sands of Iwo Jima and talking slowly to the Duke about the issues he had with his movies that bootstrap and demean Asians, be they Filipino, Chinese, Korean, Japanese or Vietnamese, and began naming the dozen, *Back to Bataan, Blood Alley,*

*Flying Leathernecks, Flying Tigers, The Green Berets, In Harm's Way, Operation Pacific, The Fighting Seabees, The Geisha and the Barbarian, They Were Expendable, Donovan's Reef.* You kept on killing us in every one of them, he looked at Sergeant Stryker in his USMC uniform, over and over. In the sky, mountain and ocean. Later, in the dawn's early light, Wing Fee asked, And you got paid for doing that?

And that's why he'd always said he did not want to be buried in Pendleton, Moon reminded Junior years later.

It had always been a struggle for the Chinese in Pendleton, more than a hundred years of it. Forced out of town for sixty years, or forced to live underground. He didn't want to be buried here. He wanted to be buried in Lewiston's public cemetery where there's a section with Chinese names and dates that go back to the nineteenth century, Junior explained later to his friends, where his wife is buried too.

Even here it's only at the northern fringe. Even in death, Moon shook his head.

Friends and family drove a near hundred miles to Idaho with their headlights on under the bluest sky. One by one they left their condolences, a flower here, a memory there and promises kept and lost. Tomorrow Moon and Junior will finish their talk about their exchange: Junior will take over the Golden Dragon for Moon; Moon will operate Junior's Unsafe and Insane fireworks business on the reservation. Together they were determined to manage their own stories while staying close to home, eastern Oregon's contested swag pitched under the rockets' red glare.

# WHITE JADE

# SECTION ONE

# 1

I am Mother. I am his mother. He is a novelist, but I am his mother writing *his* autobiography. Not just a biography, but his *au-to-bi-o-gra-phy*. He is a good writer, mind you, with prestigious awards and grants and all the rest of good table manners. So he is capable of writing his own autobiography. But he does not do autobiography. He insists he will not whore himself to sell books and write just to make the reader cry. He hammers nostalgia and the sentimental. In this his characters rarely look back—no flashback and no memory—even though all of his stories are performed in the past tense. He hates confession and self-indulgence. He thinks it is consumer-driven and therefore not art and refuses to hear that it might be otherwise, absolutely, despite almost twenty years of periodic urging by his son and wife, *my* grandson and *my* daughter-in-law.

So I am stuck with its necessity to be told, before the story lived within two entire generations disappears, that story of trans-Pacific significance which is also metaphor for understanding the huge shifts in global immigration necessitated by the wars of the twentieth century. Such dislocation, such dispossession and despair plus everything else that is relinquished. Such consequential and profound relocation of pain and power and—and there is no way of avoiding saying it here—and the arbitrary and involuntary shifting of our humanity. Then later, for those who have the stamina and luck to have survived the turn, those attempts both feeble and grandiose to repossess their lives, to begin anew, to turn to a fresh page or to start over completely, as it were, that reconstruction placing the amended heart in a new community in this exhaustive and wasteful process.

Me? I am the one left to tell the story? I am a disappeared—I died in 1944, sixty years ago. Well yes, that may well be a barrier, but it obviously has not silenced my voice, at least not in this book. The basic form of the autobiography involves a back-and-forth timewalk as often as necessary, so the real story can be told. Such a movement within the fourth dimension also occurs in fiction, or at least it should, if the truth were told.

So, if my son were to write *my* autobiography, surely relatives and historians would queue up to challenge its authenticity regardless of the volume of background research and the vetting process hired by the publisher to guarantee its accuracy and hedge it against lawsuits. Either way, one of us is bound to be the dead one, in the past or in the future-- there simply is no way around looking at it like that.

Or, there is another way of looking at all this in this massive but conventional preamble for an autobiography suggested by my consultation with Basho, Castiglione and Montaigne, Thoreau and Daniel Boone. He cannot or will not do his own autobiography because an autobiography involves *family,* and he does not do the *family thing.* Because it has to be in the first person, a performance that he seems to avoid, even in the poetry that he pretends to write. He just cannot do it, even when this is exactly the book that he has always wished he would write. He is all tied up in this in this stuff, or worse, he is pretending to look elsewhere, such as when he is faking it as a journalist and writing the occasional piece for a Seattle or San Diego newspaper just to avoid looking into his personal past. Whatever.

So then, I am doing it for him. Call it the mother's revenge, the family thing he will not do, his autobiography whether or not he thinks it is art or something less. There will be moments in this book when you might confuse my voice for his, or his for mine, but that will not matter: he is not only my first born, but my only born: his voice is my voice, and my voice is his voice, English or otherwise. You work it out. And finally, my ace of trumps, as Mother, I have privileged information.

## 2

His autobiography must begin with me in my homeland, that illusive homeland, that China where divisions both staked and cobbled by imagined differences sometimes, somehow magically turned true just enough. At least they were when I was born shortly into a new century August 18, 1908, in Tai Chung, a suburb of Suzhou, in turn a suburb of Shanghai. My parents who gave me both blood and bone and passport and currency of questionable choice or accidental birth or both—I was their only child, for whatever reason—fulfilled their life of the conventional and the privileged inherited. Which is to say that my father could go away on extended journeys and return occasionally to find everything still there, each in its right place, tended to meticulously in his absence by merchants, tradesmen, gardeners and servants. And he did do just that. Which is also to say he was never home. A mystery man, whose occasional reappearance I did not actually hear, except while being told by someone when I was old enough to listen and pretend to remember.

That probably would have been my mother, though I must say again I honestly do not remember that either, not even in this chatty timewalk unfettered and presumably omniscient. (Hey, what I could not remember that happened two years before I was five, then surely I would not remember at the age of ten, no difference, or ninety-six as I am writing this, considering that I have been dead for some sixty-one years.) Was she the one who tried to reassure me I had a father by describing the toys that he brought home for me from his last journey, that sneaky charmer? I do remember about this time I started imagining him, the him who was never there, the him as a fading bamboo rattle or teething ring that I never touched.

But in my earliest memory I do remember my mother, my mother forever in her purple, silk gown with the ideograph *home* embroidered in repeating yellow welts, her long hair pulled severely back and held pinned down in the middle by a simple, browning comb. I remember her voice, low but not soft, speaking often in short sentences, distant and nasal.

But mostly I remember her bound feet, the traditional sign that as a child she was destined to marry someone with money enough to provide someone else to do the walking for her. Every short, excruciating step defined her entire life. She was place bound—or else, the unmentionable. But maybe that was the point. It made sure the mother was always home telling lies about her husband who was never home. Ah, the significance of white arsenic powder. Whom to poison, and who to do the poisoning behind every sorrow and every smile, however small!

3

One night at the age of six when I was already in bed, my mother, her purple silk turned dark gossamer in the dimmed oil lamp, walked gingerly into my room and whispered that I would begin nursery school the next morning. Number three *amah* would walk me there in the morning and wait to walk me home in time for lunch every school day, she said. I crawled back under the covers and hushed a crazy giggle. After she left I allowed the giggle to blossom into a laugh.

A laugh that continued into the morning as I struggled with Ah San to dress myself in the fresh clean clothes that smelled of morning dew in a new life. We tugged sleeve and shoulder, heel and sock by yucky, black sock. But I won the struggle and tied the laces on my imported leather shoes that still left room to grow, that were not presents from one of my father's journeys, my mother had made sure of that.

My hand in Ah San's, it was a short walk to school. Past three courtyards and past the certified waterman with his filled wheelbarrow on his way to those other houses without running water below us, and there it was, a large brick building with windows on all sides and black shutters. If I had seen it before, as surely I must have, I do not remember except for that first moment.

After my hand was transferred into my teacher's, who was short and had a smile that would not go away all year, I tried not to think if Ah San would actually stand there all morning and wait for me at the gate, or just pretend to but go somewhere else in that time instead, I would never tell. A week later I learned to make that unspoken agreement with her not to tell, sometimes proceeded by that quickened look serving as reminder of secrets to keep from all, especially from my father who was never there, I did not forget.

Colorful chairs circled the bright room, half with boys and girls all in their starched and ironed new clothes who wished they were not there and meekly staring at the blackboard on which nothing was yet written, not even the ten basic numerals that were yet to come. Except for one, the one with the clear black eyes and a white, silk ribbon tying back her short, black hair. After a prolonged moment of looking at me, teacher introduced me as *Katherine, Katherine Ling,* that slight alteration of what I was named at home that would change my life forever. I cannot remember the names of the others now except for Wu Shiung Chien, the one who continued to look at me and at the white ribbon tying back my short, black hair and giggled. In that moment we both recognized at once we would live in that day's full promise, with that sliver of sky over us as long as friendship and life itself would permit.

4

All the children's eyes were intently focused on the blackboard the first time it was used, an early morning in the second week. With chalk in hand and a slight moment's hesitancy, her smile almost disappearing that she allowed us to see, our teacher looked into the blackboard's vault as if she was about to improvise on the galaxy's prophesies. With a firm resolve that she was not going to be dwarfed by custom or rules, she started at the top left and wrote down the ten basic numerals in Chinese from left to right, yes, from left to right, followed by their Arabic equivalents below each, every number so perfectly boxed and so perfectly spaced from each other that it will be spared the janitor's eraser for the entire year, like her smile. Then she turned to us, eyebrows raised, lips slightly parted, both palms urging us to repeat precisely after her what we had known for several years.

*Ei-Er-San-Xe...* Feeling ever so smart, we sang in unison in our best Mandarin, our second language that we only used in school. Outside, we counted everything in Shanghai-*wa*, the language of our birth.

Except for Shiung Chien. With her head slightly turned, she looked straight at teacher and appeared impatient, waiting for the next clue, anticipating the question. But, as it turned out, she already had the riddle solved even before it would be presented to us more than a year later by the next teacher.

It would be many years before I learned to survive by distinguishing between asking and not asking at the right moment. So during the courtyard recess that morning, jump rope in hand, I asked Shiung Chien outright.

Friend Katherine, she said, pointing one finger for emphasis. Those numbers, they are language. We can use them to know things and to talk to each other.

I looked at the sky behind me and in front of me, another question beginning to form on my lips.

Yes, yes, Shiung Chien repeated, even that. We can think with it.

I was not quite sure what she meant, and its presence in my mind silenced everything else that morning, that afternoon, and that evening. So I did not hear Shiung Chien as she and her *amah* turned into her avenue after school, but waved goodbye to her from a distance instead.

In nursery school, the rest of the year was less remarkable than our introduction to the numbers. Outside, Shiung Chien and I made for ourselves a mirror world to see what ours really looked like. We were all eyes more determined than before, and it was all there, all of it: a creaky floor from the forest, a floating candle beneath several moons, a mixture of speech with and without pen or brush, a jasmine, a jamb, a traveler, and, our dearest, a river with a bend in it one had reached before. Our friendship felt just like that and endured in our first year together, in her house, in mine, and in between in sunlight and in rain.

Autumn's persimmons and chestnuts disappeared quickly, but there were always oranges, sugar-dipped apples and spun cotton candy calling from vendors. The wind came up a few times in early winter, but it never reached the cold enough for snow. When spring's early yellow and small blue flowers appeared suddenly overnight in all the courtyards around us, we had already memorized the English alphabet forwards and backwards, teacher's little blossoms that would soon take her breath away.

5

F urious, Shiung Chien came out of the examination room and whispered to me, That was so stupid!

This was late May, the two of us from Tai Chung's hundreds scrubbed up and in our best clothes to be tested for admission to the few limited seats in our primary school. For this, she was accompanied by her nervous parents, both father and mother, and I by my mother, though they did not say anything to each other while we waited in line on the second floor of the city's main administration building. Shiung Chien was paraded in first, and then it was my turn.

She was right. In front of a panel of judges, all men wearing the dark blue robe of scholars, I was asked in rough Mandarin to write my name on the blackboard, first in Chinese and then in English, as if they were not pleased with the first version. Next one of them asked me to count backwards from one hundred in Chinese. By the time I got to the low eighties, another interrupted and asked me in even worse Mandarin to repeat it in English. This second trial took longer, but one of them stopped me in the high sixties and walked over and, handing me exactly one yen in coins, he asked for correct change for a dozen in eggs that were not there. I quickly counted back the fractions in halves and quarters without saying a word and without looking at him to see if it was correct.

The physical exam came next. I was directed to reach down and touch my shoe tips. Another waved two fingers and tested my eyesight. A third asked that I stand up straight and made sure I could distinguish between red and green from colored paper discs squirreled away in a small box in front of him because, as he said, they did not want to admit any flakey student into this school.

So, that was the first major step China took to cultivate its elite intelligentsia early. The decision here was final and could not be reversed. There were to be no exceptions and no appeals. This was it. Of course one could always choose self-exile and return to foment a small mini-rebellion against Beijing here or there, or, with enough money, influence or kin, meritocracy could always be circumvented.

Much later, Shiung Chien and I agreed that this exam was a precursor to the modern IQ test designed for nothing more than to eliminate the short and the tall, the fat and the skinny, so that all of us could line up in a nice neat row for the class picture of homogeneity in black and white, a hedge against the impending Japanese challenge that would surface by the time we finished college in the early 1930s.

6

Located in a very quiet neighborhood, our school was surrounded by courtyards connected by long walkways filled with pink blossoms and an puzzle of endless hedges and gates and false entrances. Intricate lattice work adorned the many doors to the main building, and as first graders to this experimental primary school of Shanghai's prestigious Fudan University, we were forbidden from using the main entrance as well as main stairwell, a reminder of the recently-recanted ideology for which this captured villa represented. This was 1925, you know, as Shiung Chien reminded me on our first day, a decade after Sun's successful revolution, at least in the coastal cities.

One unexpected consequence of this success was reflected in girls abandoning their twin pigtails and imitating the shorter styles pictured in the foreign magazines and newspapers that were beginning to appear in our stores and homes. Since Shiung Chien and I already wore our hair short, we were not sure if such a change did not reflect a mandate from these girls' parents who had a modern view of China and therefore wanted their children enrolled in this school, or if it was something the girls themselves had argued for.

In either case, most of them were dumfounded by the school's maze of walkways, even well into the second week. Many of them were late for class, and our teacher was beginning to loose his patience, suspecting that they were using it as an excuse to be perpetually late for returning to class after recess, morning and afternoon. For Shiung Chien, she had solved the riddle right away.

The secret, friend Katherine, the secret is in the number three. Never turn in the same direction more than three times.

Yes, that was it, of course. I had seen it too, but my solution rested on avoiding taking too many turns in the same direction, left or right. Above all, always keep the splurge of pink *haitan* flowers to my right on the way to the classroom building, and on the left on the way to the gatehouse. By the time the blossoms disappeared with the changing season, I had internalized these turns without thought.

Most of the experimental nature of the school was reflected in how the teacher related to his students. Because of rumors secreted from neighborhood children who attended other schools, we were surprised that a conference with a teacher most often meant a reward of silver or gold star rather than an encounter with the corporal bamboo cane. The American educator John Dewey had recently completed his visit to Shanghai, and his influential lectures led to Fudan's creation of this experimental laboratory school filled with Erecto and Lego sets, and building blocks with numbers, pictures and words, and measuring utensils—in order to make us active participants in our own learning, if you will believe that.

## 7

Thus, into this accidental world of tremendous privilege and its twin, tremendous insulation, traipsed Shiung Chien and me, hand in hand into an experimental laboratory primary school. The mornings were filled with impatience, first learning to make the darkest and thickest of ink by firmly rubbing an ink stick in tight circles against a flat stone platform covered with a light film of water, sometimes augmented with just the right amount of spittle when the teacher was not looking, ever cautious not to spill its mark onto either hand or white, cotton uniform, that telltale sign of either incompetence or carelessness, or both.

With just the right amount of ink on the brush those first two years then, we traced large letters above silhouettes boxed repetitively column after column straight up and down, page after page, booklet after booklet, part visual and vocabulary memorization, part penmanship, but mostly to trace and learn the limits of individualism within a larger social environment by connecting the dotted lines and curves. Not so experimental after all, every child in all the other, non-experimental primary schools in China was doing the exact same thing in the exact same way in the exact same moment in the morning of this country's one time zone east to west and west to east.

You know what, Friend Katherine, by the time we are done, we will have squandered nine-hundred-and-sixty hours doing this, Shiung Chien informed me during the first recess.

At that time we had not yet started arithmetic in school; that was to come later, the addition, subtraction, multiplication and division of numbers. In that morning any number beyond one hundred was unreal and purely imaginary for me. But I trusted Shiung Chien enough not to challenge such sweeping comments from her that almost always were proven ridiculously correct later. And besides—since within this autobiography I am playing loosey-goosey in my timewalk—I can skip ahead in time and say that when we were done with grade school and skip back to tell you now, we will have learned close to four thousand characters, more than enough to read any newspaper in the country. It does however, wreck havoc on the English language's handling of tense. But you see, since I am dead, remember? I do not have to play by your rules and bounds that hamper what needs to be said at the right moment for the right reason.

And I remember back in that moment, fall term of 1925, my main concern was with the number two and how it might be affected by the number three. Shiung Chien and I were friends, pals, buds, the number of two. Our parents' inevitable concern was that we did not seem to have other friends. Even our *amahs* expressed it. That seemed odd to me, born to a home with an absentee father and a circumstantial mother of dubious emotion, except for her imperial lament of accidental birth. The other children at school and in the neighborhood playgrounds were looking at us funny—their play often extended to three, four, and sometimes more. If we added a third friend, making it a total of three, would the new number *three* invariably displace the number *two* to maintain its prime identity, or would it add to it and convert it into an entirely new creation with new promises and new allegiances?

8

It is just possible that the interest in numbers both large and particular is no mere allegorical fussing in which life and death masquerade as business. The arithmetic of its utilitarian application is of course surprisingly precise in that its basic addition and subtraction provide the social glue that binds both the merchant and the draftsman. That I already knew through the exam question to make correct change for a dozen eggs for admission into this grade school, a question that Shiung Chien thought was stupid. But is it just possible that this basic precision can be ignored, or at least overlooked, when we create a world by common agreement in which the inhabited fictions appear real, however phantom they may seem at the moment? And is it just possible that these fictions become a vocabulary for challenging the boundaries of the various dimensions as we know them to be?

With this in mind then, Shiung Chien was impatient with the basic ten numbers when our nursery school teacher wrote them on the blackboard in both Chinese and Arabic. She already knew the answer, whose question would not be asked until well into the first grade. Addition. Addition every morning for months, after morning recess, so that everyone would get it right. Busy work, busy work. Repetition, repetition. Then, as if conspired with the first appearance of spring flowers and just as suddenly, its reversal went up on the blackboard, subtraction, the take away, as teacher emphasized.

By this time Shiung Chien was already entering the next stage, the fuzzy world of multiplication and division. She knew enough to compute the number of hours we were to spend tracing large letters in primary school, and it was not done by the drudgery of addition, though it was not clear to me how exactly she did it at that time. While I marveled at how small numbers can suddenly pop into large numbers, I was more curious about the hedges of plants in the courtyards about the classroom building, the edge of each leaf and the lean of every branch more demanding than before in my clearest of eyes.

# SECTION TWO

# 1

I can imagine coming out of this book and taking you by the hand to make you take a closer look at Shanghai in early 1927, can I not? A look I was completely immune to, a nine year old living an insulated life a few hours away? In retrospect, sure, the signs had always been there: at school fewer new pencils, unswept floors, smaller classes, a few teachers disappearing; and at home, less fruit, fewer vendors calling at the gate, and more caution, the silences growing wider. *Make sure you come straight home. Do not go out and play.* More and more *do nots* translated by the *amah* into *not supposed tos*. No one talked about it, not in school and not at home, not even among the *amahs* who seemed to talk about everything else. It was as if the adults had come to a mutual agreement not to talk about it. It was as if in not giving it language, it either did not exist or would disappear, a denial magnified into major proportions that would reappear several more times in this story. Ah, that magic of words that connect and separate us!

Their ignorance became our ignorance, so then it was not a surprise to us as second-graders that the teacher took the class on its annual, spring field trip to an educational landmark in Shanghai, this time Ting'an Park. It was a sunny, March morning when we boarded the bus. By the time we drove into the city, there were soldiers in the streets this spring, and more often than not, they stopped our bus at intersections. Red light, red light, soldier waving again, soldier coming onto the bus for a closer inspection again, so that the drive took twice as long as before.

Of course now I knew what we had completely missed as nine-year olds in 1927 Shanghai, the growing dissension between the students and workers against Chiang Kaishek's Guomintang, and the preparation for his imminent slaughter of his opposition. But in that time and in that place, I was captured by the millennia of plants assembled in the park. It was true. The hackberry, camphor, camellia, Mongolian yulan, Japanese white pine, Indian azalea, that 1,200-year old ginkgo, the city's first tree, its branches wide enough to provide cover for the entire class, and the gray willow, my gray willow, my sword.

In the late afternoon before we boarded the bus for our return to Tai Chung, our teacher led us to our first modern history lesson. He pointed to several blotches of dried brown-stained cobblestones by the curb and instructed us to be careful and not to step on them, that it was blood. That was all he said before quickly turning away, our mouths opened in horror and thrill. Later in secondary school I was to learn that this was the spot where a cordon of British police had fired a fusillade of bullets into the twilight of protesting workers and older students two years ago. Here was my first exposure to what violence humans are capable of inflicting upon each other and other causes of alarm to remember, and my first look past our trivial, normal lives packed with inconsequential details. It may also have been my first remembrance of time and memory and when life first began for me.

## 2

Before it was legislated into *bi-lingual*, it was more commonly known as *multi-lingual*, an integral part of everyone's education. It was assumed one knew more than one language; there was no difficulty or stigma associated with it. In school we used Mandarin most of the time, except when the teacher was not looking during recess or in the hallways or toilet; at home I spoke Mandarin with my mother and Shanghai-*wa* with Ah San because she never had a chance to learn Mandarin. But then, that was before I began to understand how language can translate itself into the politics of power and how this accumulation accelerates exponentially in the hands of a few.

So as youngsters we were not surprised when we were introduced to English in the first grade. Unlike the Chinese calligraphy that we practiced first thing in the morning, we did not have dotted lines to trace the twenty-six letters of the English alphabet. Because we used pencils to copy these letters in rows from left to right and from top to bottom, Shiung Chien liked it more than the ink repetitions in Chinese. Let's face it—she was pretty sloppy, and more often than not the heel of her right hand was smudged with wet, black ink stains from steadying it against the wet characters she had just copied as her writing moved in columns from top to bottom and from right to left in Chinese. With English, Shiung Chien could make mistakes because the writing did not leave stains, and because she could always start again after the eraser. When left alone in her adult life, she preferred English in her papers and letters, except for the rare occasions when she had time enough to write to her older relatives at home.

By the time we were in third grade, we were making fun at recess and on our way home with the growing vocabulary. We knew much of it was nonsense, but we did not care when it sounded nice, and besides, once in a while some magical connection emerged in our word play, taking us to new places and making us stop and stare.

*The boy and the girl are sitting in the red chair*
*The one talks to the other*
*"I would like to give you much more"*
*"More than the sky above the rain?"*
*The streets are empty*
*The red chair disappears*
*It is always coldest right before the sun appears*
*Is the primary teacher still smiling?*

3

When I took you by the hand to take a closer look at Shanghai in 1927 on page 101, I had made a mistake, an error in basic addition, in case you had not caught it. When I was nine years old and in the second grade, it was actually 1917, not 1927. Nine plus one-thousand-nine-hundred-and-eight equals one-thousand-nine-hundred-and-seventeen. $9 + 1908 = 1917$. Alive people making mistakes is not unique—it also happens to people who are educated and dead, sometimes the same ones. I am not embarrassed. I am not perfect. This autobiographical traipsing back and forth in time and between life and death is bound to create some chaos, not to mention my losing track of your sense of time and place.

So then, it was in 1917 that I asked you to come along on my second grade's field trip to Shanghai. Chiang Kaishek and his goons were still hoarding and running guns between Guangdong's Whampoa Military Academy that he commanded and the powerful, coastal Green Tong— and not yet in Shanghai on his murderous excursion. The blood-stained cobblestones by the school bus that our teacher led us to for my first lesson in violence and modern history were the return manifest of a ten-year leap into the future rather than a two-year rollback in time. And the leaf I snipped from the gray willow tree to press into this book was a much younger leaf from the same tree, but the same sword that would stay with me for life nevertheless. There is no difference in meaning here, only in time.

In the winter of our sixth grade, then, that is, 1921, right? Check! Our teacher was preparing the class for the three-day battery of competitive exams for admission into the same limited number of high school seats. That would be the exclusive school in Suzhou twice as far from home, with an oval, dirt track, labs stocked with German equipment, tennis courts, and all those snotty, elite boys in ties who gathered in clumps and gushed with pretended laughter thrown at girls twice as smart as they. Most of them had never learned anything in school, but had parents rich enough to hire private tutors the week before to cram them up for the exams they would forget as soon as they were over, pass or fail. Except for the essay writing part, hah, hah, hah. Here was a trap to weed out the cheaters, especially when it was repeated two days apart. But then, as before, money can buy anything, especially if one had enough of it in Shanghai's 1921 breakaway economy while the interior of China was ravaged by famine, dissension and another civil war, the second of the new century.

Shiung Chien and I never crammed for anything. We had done the work and remembered it. When we learned by special post that we had passed, we made a promise to each other that when we grew up we would never cease to be astonished by things in the world, that our energies would not be disrupted by despair or rapture, and we would never take each other too seriously. To myself, I promised I would find a silver, gray willow shoulder pin that will accompany me like the weight of home.

4

Into this modern high school twice as far from home and where the two spacious classroom buildings overlooked the tennis courts and oval, dirt track banked just at the edge where Suzhou Creek bordered the French Legation in Shanghai then, entered a new class of students mostly interested in finding some subject moving and profound enough in the next three years to build a life on. Even as a first year student, it was clear Shiung Chien had already found something enduring in mathematics and physics. For me, I saw the world through plants and ventured into botany and mathematics, though the latter was only circumstantial, just in case Shiung Chien was right about it being useful in talking with each other.

Look, look at this snippet of gray willow leaf pressed into this book from that field trip to Ting'an Park, from the willow family, one of the largest in the world. Its greens have deepened in the four years since, but its oval circumference has retained its blunt-toothed margin. It provided food for the purple emperor butterfly caterpillar, the botany teacher said, and bees counted on its pollen in early spring. As a tribe, it has learned to survive in most global conditions as long as it was close to water of some kind during the year, especially spring.

Outside the biology lab that spring of 1925 as I prepared specimen slides for a Leitz-enlarged view of capillaries and other linear aggregates of protein assembly in plants, Shanghai's turmoil was coming to a boiling point. Its sprawling metropolis of entrepreneurial chaos stamping out iron, steel and textile factories of indiscriminate labor and economy had doubled its population in my lifetime. In its position as the major port of the country's longest river that meandered sometimes roared near four thousand miles west to the Hulan Mountains near Tibet, it has claimed for itself the site for foreign nations to set its first foot down in its sinophobic march into China.

As a sixteen year old and good eyes well studied in history and politics, I knew what everyone else knew in Shanghai, that the post-encounter treaties of the last fifty years had conceded parts of the city to foreign concessions each with its own police, mansions and private parks. Our occasional outings into the city saw that these treaties provided the French, British, Japanese, Russian and Yankee mercantile imperialism a safe harbor for their gunships and sloops to creep up the river seeking China's tea, silk, and ceramics, taking back home with them indentured servants, babies and women and other forms of orientalism to obfuscate the reality of what they were doing. Except for the corporate defectors to a Standard Oil or Shell, Chesterfield or Philip Morris, most of the Chinese lived in the northern and southern shanty districts writhing under the brutal watch of the foreign-run police, factory foreman, and typhoid.

Add student idealism to this exploitive and virulent setting and there you have it, an explosive situation. So it was, that day in May, 1925, when the British police gathered and fired live rounds into a group of demonstrating workers and university students, the blood spilling onto the cobblestones. I heard the shooting and knew instantly and exactly what it was. Everyone in the lab looked up and then at the teacher, but no one said a word. A few moments later the principal came into the classroom and dismissed the class for the day.

While we waited for the bus that would take us home to Tai Chung, Shiung Chien and I read an editorial in that morning's *Shen Bao* that expressed outrage at the foreign domination of Shanghai. But there was nothing in the news that anticipated that day's events. We thought it ironic and maybe even hypercritical that these intellectuals and university students took up the position of the workers. They came from privileged or compromised backgrounds and were children of parents whose wages from these foreign companies and consortia provided for their tuition. They also lived in these same foreign legations and went to see the same Hollywood movies, separated from the real China and protected and insulated against each other as much as from the foreigners. But we also knew this severe division was part of their conquest strategy to promote a culture of betrayal, segregation and violence against each other.

We looked at each other and knew without saying it, we had difficult choices ahead of us. How would we survive? Would just a little water from the early spring rain be enough? Would we continue to dream and find there is life, after all, and places to inhabit which we can call our own, places within which we can give back something profound, for all our children? Just before the bus arrived, we looked north toward the British Legation as if expecting to see some smoke to accompany the acrid smell of gunpowder in the air. The only thing we saw was the disappearance of several teachers from the school the next day, the ominous sign of things to come.

5

The accumulation of weekly lessons and diligent daily practice including Sundays and summers did not improve my anonymous playing, so my teacher finally said at the end of five years. Yes, if I must now admit it, I had violin lessons, from a Sister Denise. How I dreaded practicing at home, consuming more time in tuning and re-tuning the instrument and preparing the bow than in putting the two together. I had a reliable enough ear for pitch, found the scales, arpeggios, voicing, crossovers, looping and bouncing pizzicato and other basic techniques easy to replicate, and learned to become quite skillful at velocity and sight-reading.

Almost dutifully, at the end of each practice session my mother would appear and applaud and utter *Bravo* in her low and harsh, nasal voice several times over as if she really meant it, mother's little darling making music, such gushing reaching way beyond for once her emotions withheld. And just as suddenly, she would shut it off and leave, as if it was a mistake, she did not mean it, or did not mean for it to extend beyond that one moment of correct, parental form. *Bravo* was also the only English word I was to hear from her, disappearing back into the dictionary when she left the room, closing the door behind her.

And then there was Sister Denise of the Immaculate Conception from Quebec, young and energetic in her starched white habit and light blue head insert, a pencil always in hand. As a newcomer to Shanghai, she also had a French-Chinese dictionary accompanying the lessons, but when it became obvious by the end of the first month that she had more problems with Shanghai-wa than I did with the violin, it was replaced with a French-English dictionary, our comfortable lesson language.

By the end of the first year I knew it. *Fine*, *Good*, and especially *Continue*, she would say, but in all of those lessons, in the end more than two hundred of them in all, she was honest and prudent and never lied and said *Excellent* or *Very good*. So I knew it long before it took her five years to finally say it in the middle of Beethoven's Second Romance in G. *Anonymous playing* meant that mother's precious little darling just did not have it, no matter how much I applied myself. Thankfully, she did not mention that occasionally my playing was slightly labored and heavy, the way Chopin's writing is often killed, one note at a time. Even doing everything correctly, I could not make music come out of those strings with any kind of voicing.

6

Over these same five years Shiung Chien was having the same problems with the piano. I was envious of her, and once complained to her that at least she did not have to lug this fancy but bulky violin case to every lesson, evoking the questioning stares along Tai Chung's streets. When our parents finally consented to the end of it in the summer before our fifth year, it was on the condition we find a suitable activities club at school to join that autumn.

Shrouded in silence, I went over the list carefully. Swim Team. Chess Club. Bridge Club. Debate Club. Literature Club. School-newspaper Club. Astronomy Club. Stamp Club. Badminton Club. Maybe astronomy. No, maybe chess. Yuck, definitely not stamps, and not literature, double yuck! Astronomy, chess. Chess, astronomy. And then Shiung Chien added bridge the next day. A game, she explained, a new game played with cards on a table. They play it over there in Shanghai, she added.

So after class in that first day of school that autumn, the two of us descended into the basement room of the second classroom building that housed the Bridge Club. Because we had to stop in the toilet for me to make a change, we were the last. In a room of some twenty students, we were the only girls. But we were used to that, after years of putting up with their arrogant and snotty exuberant exhibitions of testosterone and acne.

Since we were almost new to the club, the teacher/chaperone spent the entire first meeting explaining the game and its rules. He reminded us it was a new game, starting with four players at a square table, the opposites forming partners in a North-South and East-West compass configuration. Then he used a deck of fifty-two cards to illustrate how the game itself was played: a thorough shuffle of the deck by the dealer and its polite offer to the player on the right for a cut, always towards the dealer; a face down clockwise and sequential deal of thirteen cards to each player; the division and rank of the four suits—spades, hearts, diamonds and clubs, each from two to its highest, the ace; the competitive bidding (sometimes in codes) beginning with the dealer; the designation of trumps and later, no-trumps; the order of the play; and then the scoring, the side with the most points at the end of the game winning. Straightforward and simple enough, not requiring note taking or repetition. Then, he added, these rules are only the beginning—getting good at the game can take an entire lifetime.

As soon as we were out of the room, Shiung Chien questioned how he could know it will take a lifetime to be good at this game when the game itself was barely five-years old. A couple of the boys overheard this comment in the stairway, covered their snickering mouths with their hands and skipped back down into the clubroom, most certainly to report this challenge of authority to the teacher.

7

In late winter of my last year in high school, the Bridge Club chaperone determined that we were good enough to play in the tournament in Shanghai's British Legation Quarter the last March Sunday. He selected the best four pairs and drilled us as two teams in challenging, competitive team strategies. Shiung Chien and I were teamed with two others, whose steadfastness and occasional brilliance we both admired. We were also instructed in the rules of contest, a grueling four preliminary elimination head-to-head matches of ninety minutes each, each with sixteen duplicated deals, followed by the final two teams remaining playing thirty-two against each other. Some ten hours of play in all, with five breaks, starting at ten in the morning. When we were told that our two teams were seeded thirtieth and thirty-first in a field of thirty-two, we asked each other which the last team could have been.

At the table of the first match then, that late March, 1927, in the Bund's Grand Hotel's ballrooms, the introductions by our French Team 1 opponents were generous but formal. I sat opposite Shiung Chen keeping my eyes on the table, a low flutter in my stomach. Fortunately we had to shuffle the eight decks of cards, steadying my trembling fingers in this mechanical process. The conventional bracketing meant that our opponents, the third-seeded team of middle-aged corporate executives were pitted against the thirtieth-seeded us, still in high school, a bloodbath in the making, I thought.

Good luck, wished our opponents as we picked up our cards, as if luck had something to do with it. Shiung Chien gave me a slight, calming smile with her clear, black eyes from across the table. It's only a game, I tried to reassure myself, a game with very discrete, whole numbers. Only thirteen numbers and their potential distribution into four separate hands, I repeated to myself. No fractions. No luck. Just division, addition and subtraction, not even multiplication.

Fortunately for our inexperience, there was nothing challenging for us in the first match. French Team 1, faced with three very marginal hands, stretched them beyond their limits, for whatever strange reason. Shiung Chien and I dutifully followed suit rationally and defeated all three contracts. As our disciplined partners at table in the other ballroom holding the exact, same cards did not reach these adventurous, lucrative contracts, French Team 1 lost the match themselves, its four players and their captain last seen wagging fingers at each other and heading for the lounge.

During the early breaks from play, our chaperone beamed with congratulations but continued to caution us to play with what we were dealt, and that we did not need to make something happen, especially in these preliminary rounds. That I knew already, but I was perplexed by the French and later the Russian teams' extravagant bidding as if they wanted to take over and play every hand, even when we had more than half the face cards in the deck. I did not have the opportunity to check with Shiung Chien when I was sure they were not very good players, and suspected their display of arrogance and conceit reflected their conviction that they were better players than they were in fact. Even without knowing French, I could tell that they were laying blame against each other in their adolescent, post-mortem discussions following disastrous results. Shiung Chien and I were happy just to defend about two thirds of the hands, having decided a long time ago that we enjoyed it and had devoted a substantial portion of our practice time studying defense techniques.

Our first team, High School 1, faltered in the fourth round to British 1, nervously slipping on two vulnerable hands that were makeable, but H.S. 2, my team, survived to face the same British 1 in the final round of thirty-two deals. And yes, we were lucky, very lucky.

At precisely 7:00 P.M. then, we sat down at the head table under the multiple lights of the crystal chandeliers of the first ballroom. Our opponents were London's Mr. and Mrs. Ballard with their funny English accent, icons of British venture capital into China and the rest of Asia, and excellent bridge players as well, their names appearing often as winners in Shanghai's French and English newspapers that displayed their social calendars, including bridge, our chaperone informed us at the break. There we sat at the same table, their opponents, novice players from the local high school, majoring in mathematics, physics and botany, the color of green. They will not do anything funny like the French, American, Japanese or the Russians you've encountered in play up to this point— they've been at this much longer. They are not bold, but they are mean, their leads and carding often deceptive, always part of some imperial design, however oblique or conventional in appearance. They are good. In this match even an overtrick will matter. Play your cards; don't try to invent something spectacular.

Chairs had been provided for the galley of onlookers ringed around this table, including the Ballards' boy, a young J.G. dressed in the proper British youth attire of short, dark suit with long checkered socks. At the beginning he kept staring at his mother, urging her to hold her cards closer to the basic red of her sequined jacket. Then occasionally through the first half of this set, he seemed to be quietly clicking his tongue, as if he was not happy with the proceeding auction.

At the half we compared scores with our teammates from the other ballroom and found that the two teams were relatively even in total score, a mere three matchpoints separating us. But three points is a win, reminded our chaperone. Keep it up. Continue the good play.

Halfway into the final sixteen hands, maybe a bit delirious from the intensity of the long game, our stamina dissipating, clouded by the cigarette and cigar smoke from the onlookers, Shiung Chien took a view of the next competitive hand and made a penalty double. It worked and I suspected that we had a strong lead. (For the technical details of this hand, look to the footnote beginning on the next page.)

At the second to the last hand, Shiung Chien and I got tangled in a questionable auction and landed at a grand slam. (See the second footnote for the details.) Fortunately I found the double squeeze to make the contract's only chance. *Well played, well played,* came the generous congratulations from Mr. & Mrs. Ballard, ever the good sport. *You've won the match at this table when you played the last heart from your hand. Our partners would never reach seven hearts, and even if they had, they would not be able to make it. How did you do that? What do you call that technique?*

On the way back to Tai Chung on the bus late that night, Shiung Chien and I agreed that while it is true language, the arts, and even sports and games often reflected the cultural values inherent in their origin, they can also be beautiful, challenging and fun when they are disconnected from their ideological and political underpinnings. J.S. Bach's six French Suites are provocative, serene, beautiful and open possibilities, despite some people identifying it with some form of exclusive, national identity, French or German. So bridge too as a game can reflect the specific and narrow restrictions of its social origins and yes, certain current players continue playing the game in that tradition in a mirror perpetuating the same cultural position; but bridge as a game can also be as challenging and satisfying as what the player is willing to put into it.

---

1.

```
                    ♠ 9432
                    ♥ 9
                    ♦ QT9876
                    ♣ 75
    ♠ T875                          ♠ AJ6
    ♥ 74                            ♥ KQT5
    ♦ A                             ♦ 5432
    ♣ J98642                        ♣ KQ
                    ♠ KQ
                    ♥ AJ8632
                    ♦ KJ
                    ♣ AT3
```

| Auction: | West | North | East | South |
|---|---|---|---|---|
| | | | | 1♥ |
| | Pass | Pass | Dbl | 2♥ |
| | 3♣ | Pass | 3NT | Dbl |
| | Pass | Pass | Pass | |

Shiung Chien's penalty double of 3NT was based on an anticipated 1 trick in spades, 2 in hearts if she can avoid getting end-played, 1 in diamonds, and 1 in clubs (2 if I had the ♣-J), a total of 5, or 6, down one, at least. But in thinking through the lead and looking ahead to her hand being end-played, she decided to lead the ♦-K, hoping I had the ♦-Q or ♦-T in my hand. And it worked. Down 4 at vulnerable, + 1,100. With the – 200 when our partners got to play the hand at 2♥ undoubled in the other room, a net of + 900 points on this hand.

2.

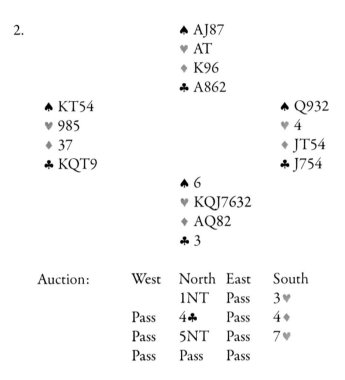

♠ AJ87
♥ AT
♦ K96
♣ A862

♠ KT54
♥ 985
♦ 37
♣ KQT9

♠ Q932
♥ 4
♦ JT54
♣ J754

♠ 6
♥ KQJ7632
♦ AQ82
♣ 3

| Auction: | West | North | East | South |
|---|---|---|---|---|
| | | 1NT | Pass | 3♥ |
| | Pass | 4♣ | Pass | 4♦ |
| | Pass | 5NT | Pass | 7♥ |
| | Pass | Pass | Pass | |

My 3♥ bid was suit establishing, followed by cue bids in clubs and diamonds. I assumed from Shiung Chien's 1NT opening and 5 NT bid that she had the top heart, as well as the ♦-K and top spade. I went for it, 7♥, a grand slam.

After the opening lead of ♣-K and Shiung Chien's hand came down, I faced some serious questions. What if the diamond suit did not split 3:3? There would not be time enough to trump out the last diamond, unless the hand with the short diamonds had only one trump. Fat chance. Was there a safe way to play and make this contract? Is there a double squeeze? I won the club in dummy, trumped a second club low in hand cautiously, remembering the warning about the Ballards' often deceptive leads. Then to dummy's ♥-T before trumping a third club high, leading a trump to the ace, back to hand with the diamond ace and picking up the last trump and playing diamonds until I discovered it did not break 3:3. So I played another trump to reach this position:

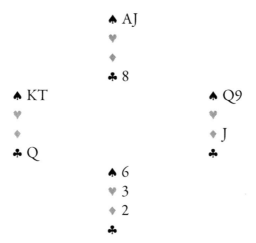

♠ AJ
♥
♦
♣ 8

♠ KT                  ♠ Q9
♥                        ♥
♦                        ♦ J
♣ Q                   ♣

♠ 6
♥ 3
♦ 2
♣

On the play of the last heart from my hand, the opponents were doomed. West could not protect both the spade and club suits, and east both the spade and diamond suits. If Mr. Ballard discarded his last club, my club in dummy would be good. If he discarded a low spade, his ♠-K would be pickled. If Mrs. Ballard discarded her good ♦-J on my heart to protect her ♠-Q, then my ♦-2 would be good. Either way, the play of the last heart from my hand squeezed both opponents and guaranteed me the last three tricks, thirteen in all, making the grand slam and a + 2,210 points. With the Ballards' partners in the other ballroom reaching 6♥ with the same hand and making 6, - 1,430 for us, for a net of + 780 for High School 2 winning the tournament seeded thirty in the field.

## 8

Two weeks later Ah San warned that the stores in Shanghai were closed, the streets getting empty. Everyone was getting edgy and quiet, even the songbirds in Tai Chung's parks several miles away. Soon Generalissimo Chiang Kaishek's troops started making random sweeps of the city, stopping passersby and checking out their political identities. Possession of *Shen Bo*, Shanghai's largest daily newspaper that leaned slightly to the left of center, was alone sufficient evidence for arrest, torture, imprisonment, exile, or execution.

We had learned about these soldiers in our junior year history classes. At the Whampoa Military Academy in the south, principal Chiang had distinguished himself by instituting a culture of collective responsibility for the school's cadets. If anyone in a military unit disobeyed an order, the entire unit would be executed, he lectured, an extraordinarily steep expectation considering that his troops were not organized, and were mainly made up of poorly fed, badly paid, and underarmed conscripts dredged up mostly from the impoverished rural areas. So on April 12 it was not a surprise to anyone in Shanghai when Chiang ordered the immediate execution of every communist in the city.

It started with the bloody betrayal and targeted killing of *Shen Bo*'s editor and quickly turned into an all-out campaign aimed at exterminating every Chinese in the city suspected of being a communist, whether they were Chinese or Russian Communist Party members or unionized workers, sympathetic students or intellectuals restless about their second class status in their own country. Even the five international legations were not exempted from this brutal search. By the second day, those foreign consulates alarmed enough by the indiscriminate bloodletting began escorting their citizens onto their ships in the harbor for safety.

The executions and noise of the machine guns and smoke from small fires continued for weeks and were witnessed by all in Tai Chung.

Several years later in the United States, my husband was to tell me that Generalissimo Chiang had caught Zhou Enlai—one of the top CCP's leaders who would later become the Republic of China's first premiere—in the first week that April and had him imprisoned. Later in the spring of 1933 in a San Francisco restaurant, my husband-to-be related to both Shiung Chien and me that as president of Fudan University and having grown up in the same closely-knit Fujian Province as Chiang, as well as the powerful and violent Green Tong itself (none of whom could speak a passable Mandarin sentence), he cajoled and shamed Chiang into releasing Zhou. For me at that moment, however, I was beginning to see Shanghai as a place that I would associate with personal awakenings, despair and loss. I am exhausted.

# SECTION THREE

# 1

At this point I am exhausted from describing these personal and startling narratives set in the Shanghai of 1925 and 1927. I have waited near eighty years to tell this part of the story. Sometimes the voice has been urgent, sometimes withdrawn and reflective, and sometimes in the gaps, the silence of midnight crying. On another level, I want you to hear my voice and remember it, so that you will recognize it in a crowd, or on the telephone years from now, and maybe even put a face to it. For now however, I must return to that point before it is stolen like a misplaced umbrella for someone else's story, so it won't drift back in later on in the book, remembered in an inappropriate and embarrassing moment.

Late summer of 1927 then. The Generalissimo had seized all of Shanghai in a bloody coup, and some fifty miles away in Tai Chung, Shiung Chien and I were getting ready to go to Central University in Nanjing. I had decided to trim my hair shorter and had it permed in a Suzhou saloon, a flapper cut just long enough to leave a shock of black hanging over my right eyebrow. The few clothes we bought on the same trip were practical and easy to wash. We found and exchanged gifts for each other, bracelets made from interlocking pieces of white jade, a sign of peace, friendship and long life. I did not find a silver willow pin for myself. That night I felt at long last I was leaving home, at the age of nineteen, and I was ready for it.

## 2

Beautiful and mythical Nanjing, the world's first city, protected by a coiling dragon and crouching tiger, but in its more realistic description, it is one of the Long River's Four Smokestacks. Coming from Shanghai, Shiung Chien and I were used to that humidity, even in early autumn when we took that short train ride upriver to register for classes at Central University. Both of us were excited, our curiosity anticipating worlds opening up.

But everything was a disappointment that first day: the dormitory, the lines for everything, the dining room, the food, and the politics.

We had expected to have roommates in the girls' dormitory, but not those double-tiered bunk beds that were too short for me, the two sets taking up most of the room. The rest of the space was occupied by two small desks the four of us had to share. Shiung Chien thought they were even smaller than the desks in our Tai Chung high school. The only relief of the day came in meeting our roommates, two very smart, young women with a sense of humor, one from distant Chengdu and the other Changchun. Xiaoming from Chengdu pantomimed a walk from the door to the window, bumping into the bunk beds from side to side in comic exaggeration. And Elizabeth suggested we withhold our judgment until we had seen the common washroom, which turned out to be even smaller than our bedroom, and it had to be shared by everyone on the floor, about thirty in all, and double as our laundry room.

We spent the entire afternoon in a long line to meet with our assigned adviser before registering. When we finally met him, a frail and retired professor with kind eyes who kept on nodding his head, we decided just to get his trembling signature on our permission forms and leave quickly in case he would expire right there in front of us.

We met Elizabeth and Xiaoming in the long dining hall. It was painfully noisy, the line long, and the food, well, the food. Our first time away from home, the four of us thought the food too spicy, not spicy enough, the rice too firm, the rice not firm and white enough. The loud and equally rowdy-looking cooks in their blue uniforms and folding white hats slammed inexact portions of food into our metal *fanghe*s and dared us to complain or whine with their lewd stares.

There was no avoiding it. The only empty seats left in the dining hall were at a table around which several students were deep in political discussion and yelling at each other. One of them said that just when he thought he had escaped the corruption and graft of the new government under Chiang Kaishek by coming to school here, he heard a report Chiang was planning on moving the national capitol from Beijing to Nanjing. Another said that made sense, since Old Peanut Head could not speak a sentence of Mandarin and besides, in Nanjing he would be reconnected with the powerful, coastal Green Tong. No, he wanted to distance the new government from the feudalism and dynastic bureaucracy of old Beijing, these are his reasons. Hey, you moron, the dynasties in Nanjing go back to the third century, did you not know?

Xiaoming whispered for us to keep quiet. She should know, coming from that northern, border province with its long history of political intrigue, oppression and betrayal. There are GMT agents here pretending to be students who will take down your name and report you, she warned. Some will even pretend to be your friend, and then turn you in. Be careful what newspapers you read and what books you borrow from the library. Your letters will be opened. Shiung Chien and I listened carefully to all of this and ate the remaining of our rice too firm or not firm enough in silence. I was beginning to doubt if I were really ready for it.

3

Raising myself up on one elbow on my lower bunk bed on a rare lazy Sunday morning, I laughed at the disorganization and chaos around the room. Wet clothes from Saturday night's washing ritual were draped over taut hemp lines randomly drawn from bedpost to bedpost. Stacks of books and notepads cluttered everywhere, the floor, the barely visible two desks, the beds, Shiung Chien's thick quantum mechanics textbook propping open the window, and old, graded assignments and tests bulging from the suitcases hidden beneath the beds. Stretching my neck to look around someone's hanging sweater at Xiaoming's bed, I could not tell where the books and papers ended and where her body began. The four of us had become too serious in our studies—we must take a break. After all, the first year was almost finished.

Shiung Chien had immersed herself in particle physics, quantum mechanics and classical dynamics, and I was registered for lectures and demonstration experiments in molecular biology, vascular physiology and floral evolution. Xiaoming and Elizabeth were similarly occupied with chemistry and mathematics.

We put on our best clothes, helped each other with our hair, and deep from our suitcases exchanged tubes of lipstick. We jumped on Xiaoming when she produced something called *Helene Curtis Eyeliner,* first learning to use it and then interrogating her on finding such a cosmetic item in Changchun. When she said she had bought it in the port of Harbin frequented by merchant and naval sailors from the world over, our teasing only got worse.

Past the main gates of the university, we followed each other in twos into the streets of Nanjing, the colors of the city of lakes, rivers and hills exploding in that June's sunlight, bring with us our pooled, leftover money. We decided the recently constructed mausoleum on Zijin Shan to honor our revolution's founder Dr. Sun, or the airfield with the much heralded newly-arrived American aircraft that was of interest to Shiung Chien were both too far for us to walk, and instead meandered slowly toward Xuanhu Lake. For the first time in several years in memory I was happy to just bask in the beauty of the many, intoxicating colors of the plants in their blossomed brilliance and hedged secrets, rather than identify the taxonomy and morphology of each.

We stood at the steps leading to the fancy hotel on the lake guarded by two uniformed GMT soldiers with rifles and laced leggings at each of the entrance stone lions, and counted enough money for our first beer and a pack of Chesterfield cigarettes, rather than spend it on a good meal in a less expensive restaurant away from the lake. This was to be our special day, we reminded ourselves; we can always eat another time.

The waiters and bartenders in the lounge were quite abrupt and rude, most dismayed that four very young and quite possibly cheap-looking Chinese ladies had mistakenly walked at the wrong time of day into their hotel frequented by foreigners. Yes of course, we had heard stories about this strange form of lateral violence, and was beginning to wonder if we were not going to be served in our own country and asked to leave. But their demeanor changed the instant two western men got up and made room for us to join them at their low table. They were from Germany, and they would like to meet some Chinese girls, they said in the worst accented English I was to ever hear in my lifetime, quite possibly the way I imagined Chiang and others from Fujian Province would sound in Mandarin. We looked at each other in agreement, thanked them and found our own table close to the window overlooking the deep-blue lake, its armfuls of lilacs separating its wisteria arbors, and the purple mountains behind them reaching into the fourth dimension.

4

At the beginning of our last year at Central, about one hundred recently graduated students from all over China came to campus to take the national exam that would qualify a handful of them for the Boxer Rebellion Indemnity Scholarship and send them to the top graduate schools in the United States. All men, clutching their university diplomas and testimonials for two years of dedicated service, they appeared terrified, milling about the quadrangle before the exam and not speaking to each other. Two of our lecture halls were appropriated for this one-day exam.

The university officials had informed us that all four of us had qualified to take this exam because of our rank in class and our geographical origin. But we had to decide by the end of the week if we wanted to be included.

We talked about it and talked about it. It was all coming out now. The four of us had kept quiet ever since that warning in the dining hall three years ago, our breaths sucked in and our mouths shut. But we have kept our ears to the ground, and we know, we know. We were not just privileged students on our way to the government's university's rice-bowl for life, Helene Curtis products in hand.

We knew about the history of the scholarship, that it grew out of President Roosevelt's refusal to accept China's usury payment to the U.S. for damages to American property in China during the ill-fated Boxer Rebellion. He asked that the excess be returned, trade deficit or no trade deficit—he argued that if Americans wanted China's tea, silk and ceramics, then the consumer will just have to pay for them, and the Yankee mercantilist would have to find some honest way to sell something to the Chinese that they'll want, the hard way. So a compromise was reached and the scholarship fund established despite China's protest that the money was more needed by the government for the support of its faltering civil infrastructure.

Shiung Chien was particularly suspicious of the implications of the GMT's administrative rules of this scholarship, given its widely known repressive activities in the name of national unification and homeland security, beginning with the extermination of the Chinese Communist Party in Shanghai three years ago. When we come back, would we have to work for the government, she asked.

Coming from Jilin Province—a veritable doormat that had somehow survived a long history of foreign invasion and occupation from all points of the compass—Xiaoming took a more accommodating view. Let's face it, she asked, who else would give her a job when she returned with an advanced degree in numbers theory besides a government supported school? With the Boxer scholarship, we would be assured of access to the top positions and our careers would be guaranteed. If she wanted research autonomy, she would do better to stay in America where her education would not be wasted.

Elizabeth was more skeptical, and argued that while it might appear our chances might be better in America, realistically she believed the chances that an American university or American company would give us an opportunity to teach or conduct research there are slim. She had heard that the American government wanted this scholarship to control the intellect and spirit of China's future leaders. Returning is an underlying design of this program.

We were faced with a dilemma, one that haunted us until the four of decided independently and informed the university without telling each other at the end of the week that we will take our chances and go on our own without the GMT's watchful sponsorship and the American government's shepherding.

5

Chaos swooped over our last year on campus. There were student protests almost every week, sometimes followed by disappearances. Occasionally the same GMT Curtiss Hawk would splutter low, taking photographs of the demonstrators for future reference. We were advised to never look up at the grinding noise of the approaching biplane, a dying chicken trying to cough, lest our faces appear in the wrong story. In the spring, Ministry of Propaganda officials invited selected student leaders to a personal audience with the Generalissimo, who asked the students for patience and heaped upon them reassurances, promises of a bright future with the GMT government, ending in a group photograph with them. They left with a sense of great accomplishment and pride that upon graduation they would be included in the government's plans for the reconstruction of China.

The four of us were not so sure. Expecting nothing, we rooted among the library's catalogues and ended applying to three schools, University of Chicago, Massachusetts Institute of Technology, and the University of California.

6

By the time Shiung Chien and I struggled with our suitcases toward the wharf in Shanghai bound for our voyage to the United States in August, there were armed soldiers everywhere, including belted machine guns in the city's major intersections and along the waterfront. Japan had been heralding the necessity of a pan-Asian resistance of Western imperialism, and appointed itself to provide the leadership for such a rejection. China was not so sure, and was preparing for a Japanese invasion from the north through Korea.

These soldiers did not chatter among themselves as before, and gestured toward the impossibility of it all. Most of them were the country's discarded youth, and, wearing helmets too large or too small or without, they appeared to be untrained conscripts in whose unwashed bodies bounded the future of a nation that could not provide them any option in life other than as canon fodder in scurrilous and perpetual violence. Eyes half closed, Shiung Chien and I could not look at each other as we passed them, our shoulders heavy with the shame of the nation and ourselves.

We could not look at each other also because Xiaoming and Elizabeth were not with us. Disregarding letters from home pleading and praying for her to Go, go now, our future is in your future in America, Elizabeth decided in her heart of hearts she was just an ordinary person and returned to Changchun to be with her family awaiting the imminent invasion and said nothing more. And without explanation, Elizabeth just said I'm going back to Chengdu, and we knew what she meant without rearranging a single word.

We turned around for a last goodbye look at Shiung Chien's waving parents and my silent mother in the distance, and faced *President Jackson's* steward with our embarking papers. (I can tell you here, now, because it is necessary. We did not know then on that wharf in 1931, we did not know that we would never see them again, not in my lifetime.) Then, following a voice penetrating both skin and bone, my father ran up to us. Just in time to say goodbye to you, he blustered. Absentee father for twenty-three years, showed up to say goodbye to his only child, a daughter he would see even less after that moment. Angry, hurt, pleased and angry again, I could barely nod. In the silence, Shiung Chien looked away to the stern of the ocean liner. In that moment I accepted how much I had hated him, his name, the name of father in any language, *Ba-Ba,* traceless in my throat in all those years.

# SECTION FOUR

# 1

Since I do not possess the omniscience to be everywhere at once, I can only narrate and interpret events in whose time and place I was present—I just can't be in two places at once, sorry, not even in death. For anything else, I have to rely on second and third hand sources and, of course, on my primary informant, my son, the writer.

So for now I must rely on the *San Francisco Chronicle* for reports filed by correspondents who were hopefully witnesses on the scene and truthful. In September, the receding Long River flood and a raging, communist revolt in Jiangxi Province. In September, Japan's march into the north precipitated a national boycott of classes by hundreds of thousands of students protesting both the invasion of China and GMT's failure to respond seriously to it. The students were angry enough that ten days later a few from Nanjing's universities kidnapped the GMT's foreign minister and roughed him up on suspicion he was a traitor.

The meeting of the small UC's Chinese Students Association for once did not focus on a social activity but had an political agenda, a determination for activism that would somehow assuage our collective guilt for having escaped—or at least been excluded—from participating in and in many cases dying in our homeland's trials. After reading these devastating reports, some were crying; some wanted to go home; some accused; some wanted to storm the Japanese consulate in San Francisco the very next day. In the end, nothing was resolved below the raised, excited voices. For me, aside from my continuing anxiety about Xiaoming and her family in Changchun, this student fixation on *homeland* was day-by-day becoming less tolerable and more abstract, beginning when Shiung Chien and I sailed from Shanghai on the *President Jackson* a month ago. After the final dumpling disappeared, everyone left without saying a word, taking their woks and chopsticks with them.

On my way back to my apartment that night, the graduate students' descriptions of the man my adviser Professor E. C. Tolman had assigned me to as research assistant trailed in my steps. He was firm and did not waver, because that would compromise his independence, hah, hah; he had kind eyes, so be careful; he did not have a private life, he lived in his lab, so be more careful, hah, hah; he received his Ph.D. in philosophy from UC at the age of twenty-five; look at what the man called himself, *Zing Yang*, Enduring Mission, hah, hah; he was the president of the prestigious Fudan University when he was twenty-six; the guy was stuck up, he did not mix with them; he had five brilliant publications before he was twenty-five; he saw a GMT agent in every Chinese in Berkeley, be careful, hah, hah; he was handsome and wore expensive suits and ties, be careful; he wore a cue until he cut it in a ceremonial protest when he was still in elementary school; and he had three young children left in Shanghai from a wife leftover from a prearranged feudal marriage in his hometown of Shantou, a fishing village, mind you.

At the doorway to my building, I wanted to step aside to think about what to anticipate in my meeting with Professor Zing Yang Kwok the next day, and wondered about the chance I had taken in coming here to America. Instead I was worrying about Shiung Chien who was not at this meeting tonight. We had been seeing less of each other, and she appeared to be spending more time in her lab, having signed up for classes in time invariance, parity symmetry, double beta decay and a voyage to Jupiter.

# 2

Startled, Professor Kwok looked up at me. In his white lab coat and embroidered silk tie, he had been looking out the window of his psychobiology lab, perhaps admiring the morning sunlight on Berkeley's hillsides. Irritatingly quiet, formal and distracted, he gestured for me to sit down on a nearby stool. So, those graduate students were beginning to be right last night.

But his first words surprised me when he voiced concern for my friends' and family's safety in a city wracked by civil unrest as well as war. I thanked him and got out a pencil and notepad, ready to jot down my duties as his laboratory assistant. He looked at my jade bracelet for a moment, turned and walked back to the window. Slowly, as if to make himself clear or to give me time to take it all down, he proceeded to outline my duties.

Keep the lab neat and tidy. Oversee the supplies will not run out. When you leave, make sure all the microscopes are covered, all the lights out, and doors locked. Complete requisition forms for breakage, over there, on that table by the door, he said still without turning around. Your key is there too. In small handwriting, I wrote down *research assistant = slave* in the margin, and underneath it underlined *slave, lab rat, lab maid*. Grade tests twice a term, he continued. Time permitting, prepare avian embryo slides for demonstration in graduate seminar on laboratory techniques. *Low-level lab tech.* Next, be cautious of salmonella. Instead of jotting it down, I looked up at him, but he was secretive, still looking out the window. A longer pause this time before he finally turned around from the window, the light behind him. There was the slight hint of a smile through his wire-framed glasses when he said—again in the same monotonous and quiet voice—that's not true; I was just seeing if you were paying attention.

Then the meeting was over. He wished me a good year and formally handed me the key, showed me to the door, gently closing it behind me, its brass latch clicking into its metal locket, the entire interview taking less time than it does for you to read this report, word for word, even with interruption. That was it, period.

On my way to the library, my head down, I was so furious I had a hissy fit. He had not even said *Hello,* our first meeting. Salmonella. Warning me about bacterial infection in chicken embryos, as if I didn't know anything. Rude, checking me out like that, not to mention Central University's curriculum. Arrogant, elitist, stuck up snob. Why did he not just ask me outright if I knew enough to know? He was from Fujian Province, it made sense then. Sure, like Generalissimo Chiang Kaishek, the bandit, the inheritor of the wretched Provisional Presidency of the Republic of China, both of them were from Fujian Province. The elitist snobs. Like him, Professor Zing Yang Kwok or whatever his real name was, he could not even cuss in Mandarin, I bet, least of all speak a passable sentence in it. Sure, Shantou, a small fishing village, that made sense. The two of them probably lived in the same neighborhood and went to the same school, the school of arrogant snobs who contracted an early case of salmonella and did not even know it playing pirates on the beach as friends. And his maroon, silk tie with its raised embroidery in imperial yellow!

When I finally looked up from my ranting, I found myself in front of the English building, my eyelids stuck together.

## 3

There, in a very small store up on Telegraph Avenue two blocks returning with a book from Cody's, there in the window's imploring shadow and light, the pin. The older women inside with the beautiful silver hairpins and necklace smiled and asked who I was. I told her I was a student from Shanghai, China, from the other side of the Pacific Ocean, pointing to the west. Then she said she was a Hopi-Laguna, but lived in Santa Fe, a Lamson.

She rubbed the pin clear with her fingers, removed the price sticker and presented it to me, both palms up. This was it, that silver, gray willow leaf, my life's keep—its etched pinnate lines tracing the weight of its home, its margins shaped into the same oval as that snippet tucked into this book from my second grade (am I getting this right this time?) field trip. I must have looked at it for many moments before I asked her for its price.

This had been waiting for me, she said. There was no price, this gift from the Three Mesas of her home. When she pinned it over my heart, I put a hand over hers to thank her. She looked over at the window and told me someone was waiting for me. I turned, and there was Professor Kwok, the pirate, silk tie flying in the wind and smiling *Ho Ho Ho and a bottle of rum.*

4

At this small café with teas from the East, I decided on *pu er*. He waited and asked for chrysanthemum, catching my surprise. Did I expect him to order some obscure oolong from Fujian Province, he asked, smiling? Then he waved off my coins when I was preparing to pay the cashier who had kept her eyes on us from the moment we walked in the door, insisting I was still an underpaid and exploited graduate student.

There, with fading, yellow flower petals floating in his cup, he looked across the small table at me and said he was thankful for my good help in the lab and inquired if I was comfortably settled in and about my family and friends, distinctively interested. A little nervous in this unusual setting and mindful of the graduate students' warning to be careful, yes, I said something vague about Tai Chung and Suzhou, following botanical studies at Nanjing's Central University and *President Jackson* and how big the Pacific Ocean was to sail on.

Then he looked at my bracelet and said he liked my new pin. Surprised again—I thought he had not even noticed me in his lab before, much less what I wore. Embarrassed, my face must have flushed as I covered my sword with my left hand, finally raising the white flag. Here was a very nice man who away from his lab appeared to be quite human and normal, a breath of fresh air. He also said he was from a small village on the Han River, near Shantou. So he didn't play pirates with Chiang on the beach, it seemed. But that did not last long.

As if I were not already familiar with his work, he claimed he was against instinct, which he described as armchair psychology. But he was not a behaviorist either, or against theory, preferring to see himself as a scientist interested in the hard-core investigation of the human developmental processes, whether they were anatomical, physiological or behavioral. Because there was no name for that yet, he insisted, his work was being shoved into the wrong pigeonholes, as it were, he added.

The cashier continued to look at us on our way out, her head slightly tilted. Professor Kwok, no, sorry, Zing Yang by now, helped me on with my coat and asked if I had thought he was going to discuss the differences in the teas from Yunnan, Fujian and Hainan Island? All I could say was no, not necessarily, my flag still up.

## 5

That spring for some reason I still don't know, I started writing letters.*

April 14, 1933
My dear Shiung Chien,
You must be very busy with your studies. I am too. I long for our chats, our friendship. You are very lucky, you do not have to teach or be someone's research assistant. You can devote all your attention to your studies.

I have told Professor Kwok the pirate about our friendship. He has invited you to join us for a dinner in San Francisco this Friday or Saturday. I hope your work will allow you to enjoy this outing to the city.

He is actually quite nice, not a short monkey rice-eater from south of the river who does not speak Mandarin.

Affectionately,
Your friend Katherine

---

* Almost exactly forty years after my death, Shiung Chien tracked my son Yahli to a university in the Pacific Northwest and mailed him all of my letters, including this one.

6

At this moment at least China's index of war with Japan was lowered by the shaky Tanggu Truce brokered by Italy, France, Great Britain and the United States, ceding a good portion of northern China to Japan, an area over whose proprietorship blood had been steadily spilling over the last four centuries.

The three of us were seated at a corner, window table with fresh daffodils. It was early, still light enough to see the Bay and a section of the pink, suspension bridge from Brandy's. Stirring her steaming, fish ball soup seasoned with sprigs of fresh spinach, Shiung Chien looked comfortable with us, and that was important for me. But Zing Yang—who had selected this restaurant while claiming in his usual imperative English construction that the best Chinese cooking can be found in San Francisco and Vancouver—Zing Yang continued to be disturbed by the GMT's vigorous elimination of dissension in Nanjing and Jiangxi Province. I was beginning to feel that things were simpler between us now, moved in from the edge, and admired his commitment to the necessity of the independence of inquiry.

By the time the pork, cabbage, mushroom and egg stir-fry was brought to the table, Zing Yang was still talking about 1927 Shanghai. Shiung Chien and I looked at each other. Then I reached over and put a hand on his arm. He looked up at me and understood enough was enough, that though our life might pale against the significant and shattering other across the six-thousand mile wide Pacific Ocean, our life was also a life, and we must allow time for it.

7

What a strange way of looking at things, I thought to myself. Here was a man who hung up his tie first before unbuttoning his shirt, and he's asking me to move to the University of Rochester with him as his wife. We need to make a collective agreement, he said, to make our life easier, so people won't ask and we won't tell, he added. He has got to be kidding.

It will only be for a year at Rochester, before an appointment at Yale's Osborn Zoological Laboratory, and then the embryo lab at the Carnegie Institution of Washington. And become what, a research gypsy going from one institute to the next? Maybe Elizabeth was right in her doubts an American university would give a permanent appointment to a Chinese scientist, in spite of Z.Y.'s brilliant publication record—as one critic described it, he had out-Watsoned Watson, and probably Pavlov and Skinner and me too in the process.

No, no, no, he insisted. In a developing field, he needed these different labs for their special equipment and libraries. And what if I said no, I doubt that, will that get me anywhere? So instead I asked what would I do in Rochester, in New Haven, in Washington? He had the answer for that too. We will work together; I will be his assistant.

Oh yes, I will play the flute on the radio, *Blue days, all of them gone; nothing but blue skies, from now on*. Oh yes, I will be wife, I will be mistress. Even though the timing was perfect, my questions were too much to ask of him at that moment. But I remember them enough to repeat them exactly here. What will happen when the wife say no and the mistress say yes? What will happen when the wife say yes and the mistress say no? What will happen when both say no? And what will happen when both say yes? Will it get me anywhere if I said no then? I did not let him turn the lights out, but he kept his eyes closed throughout.

8

**B**y the middle of the next year at Berkeley, Shiung Chien completed the requirements for her degree. Under the supervision of Ernest Lawrence, the cyclotron inventor, her concentration in high-energy physics challenged the concept of left-right models attached to parity symmetry in the fifth dimension.

I had read her ten-page dissertation over tea one afternoon before her final exam, just the two of us, and now remember nothing more than the beautiful equations on the page. What I remember more were our words for each other, old friends about to leave each other, friends marking companionship beginning with nursery school, then primary and secondary schools, then college, and now, some six-thousand miles from our first home, in the same graduate school in a new country of our fourth year.

For the first time in twenty-one years, our lives would begin to appear in different mirrors and separate photographs. The very air we breathe in the morning will be different, in a different time zone, in different lives. There will be great sadness, a loss, an empty space. We looked at our bracelets, gifts to each other, like our lives, and now, the tear of tears. Our parting promise to each other borrowed part of an old Chinese proverb— yes, we were turning a page, but we will remain in the same book.

A week later, before the Christmas recess, she started packing for her appointment at Columbia. In celebration, Zing Yang and I took her out to dinner. We were getting ready to leave for Rochester too. Picking at the last of his Alaskan king crab, Zing Yang looked at Shiung Chien with respect, and joked that she would need a classroom with blackboards on three walls to teach at Columbia. There was very little evidence left of the past then, a hiatus waiting for the next newspaper headline, *Nothing but blue skies* in my ear.

9

In West Haven two winters later, with Zing Yang away in his lab almost sixteen hours a week, seven days a day examining avian embryonic developmental behavior that by then did not need my assistance anymore, I started attending a few lectures again, reading novels by American writers and listening to Shakespearean plays on the radio on Monday evenings, following the script on my lap. The university community around us was very generous, opening their homes for parties and dinners. At one of them I accepted exciting invitations to join both the Yale Dames and American Association of University Women.

My association with the YD did not last long, after a few afternoon tea parties extended into very disappointing bridge games. Charles Goren introduced his popular point-count method to the world of bridge in his book *Winning Bridge Made Easy* the year before—four for aces, three for kings, two for queens, one for jacks, as well as three for voids, two for singletons and a questionable one for doubleton. These YD players had memorized it, at least the point-count, as well as some rudimentary elements of its bidding system in the beginning of the best-seller. But pity, all that meant to them was now it became easier for them to be poor players.

The newspaper and radio reports in the second week in December brought news of Japan's massacre of Nanjing. Since the A.A.U.W. had asked me to give a talk on my impressions of it, I spent a few days preparing. Zing Yang was not much help because he was too angry to be coherent, ranting not only against the Japanese invaders, but also against the failure of GMT to concentrate its military forces against the perpetrators. He was equally severe on the refusal of the United States to foresee a common enemy and directly join China's resistance.

First the reported numbers were staggering, as well as some of the acts attributed to the Japanese soldiers away from home, the unimaginable slaughter, destruction, raping and looting. I did not think these reports were reliable since they did not come from eyewitness correspondents who had been evacuated from Nanjing the week before, but from third hand sources whose versions were bound to have been severely edited by publishers with very specific political and propaganda agendas. So I focused my talk on a distanced and imagined post-war dialogue among sensible persons from both China and Japan about what really happened at Nanjing.

The scale of the numbers would not be a good place to begin, I started my presentation. To get the real number of how many died, we would have to ask those who got killed, a basic impossibility. No, no, don't look away—this is not nonsense, but an honest attempt to understand what really happened the week of December 10. Some Japanese would argue that the Nanjing residents carried out a scorch-earth policy of their own, that the GMT soldiers did their share of the looting before abandoning the city, and a few would even deny the Rape of Nanjing happened at all. Would the world formulate a post-war expectation that soldiers brutally engaged in the act of sanctioned killing should be held to a higher moral standard?

Assuming China won the war, would there be an international military tribunal that would look at hard evidence—battle records from both sides, civilian and soldier diaries--and come to fair conclusions against the Japanese, the loser of the war? And who would be held responsible, the person spewing the words or the person aiming the rifle? And what about those in between? Would it come down to who fired the bullet and who lowered the sword, while the rest of us watched in silence and wagged our finger?

My presentation was not well received by the A.A.U.W. Yale had long historical ties to China through its Yale-in-China missions, and I had misinterpreted the nature of their request to present my take on what happened in Nanjing. They wanted confirmation more than understanding. They wanted confirmation; interpretation from a tall, Chinese lady they thought was smart and elegant who had gone to college in Nanjing less than ten years ago, was tantamount to eyewitness pleading that they must be more vigilant and further dedicate their activities to saving the now more-battered and more-savaged spirit of China.

Zing Yang was so furious with me when he found out about their disappointment on the same day that he had fewer than a dozen words to say about it. When he got home late that night, he did not say a single word to me. At the beginning of dinner, he lifted his fork, then changed his mind and set it back down to the side of his plate. He looked at me and asked if I had forgotten that these people help write U.S. foreign policy for Washington.

# 10

There was nothing I could say that night. My presentation on post-war convergence and mending and what can be learned from our mistakes was made at the wrong time, and at the wrong place, Yale University, New Haven, Connecticut. But what happened in Nanjing to whatever ambiguous degree of truth was to be overshadowed by reports coming out of Changchun. The editors at *Time, Newsweek, Life* and all those dynastic publications of William Randolph Hearst and Henry Luce—who was after all the scion of American missionaries in China—ratcheted up their language, from *The Rape of Nanjing* to the *Factories of Death*.

Led by Units 731, 100 and 516 of the Japanese Imperial Medical Corps, they developed and tested biological and chemical agents —anthrax, Bubonic plague, typhoid, syphilis, you name it—another instance in which the independence of scientific research for humanitarian purposes was compromised or at least leased for military objectives. Their facilities were known as lumber mills, and local, unsuspecting civilian subjects who became their guinea pigs were referred to as *logs*.

As much as I was cautious of the reports' propaganda value and their editorial distortions, there must have been some basis of truth in their origins, I thought, attaching a three-cent, purple George Washington stamp on my letter to Shiung Chien.

> February 14, 1938
> My dear Shiung Chien,
> At this moment when we are both thinking about Elizabeth and the biological and chemical testing in Changchun, we must continue to believe there is hope in tomorrow and be firm in our resolve to do everything we can to prevent its re-petition.

Professor Kwok the pirate continues to work long hours in the lab on his embryo studies, and I have been busy reading many American novels from the library.

I hope your teaching and research will allow you to come up here for a weekend visit soon. Though small, our house has a very comfortable guest room for you as always.

Affectionately,
Your friend Katherine

# 11

There then, I am Mother, the beginning of beginnings, everyone's mother, this common body, this shared vessel, pushing him into bone and pushing him into skin that will bound him, this other me, this blood of my blood. All my ten fingers tightened white, clutching the edge of my firmament where each breath pushed light and pushed darkness and every biting silence in between extending up below from my depths.

Snowing lightly outside the window in that mid-January winter into the world like everyone else whose journey was already half over at this beginning, this baby, my baby, my strength, my Yahli, I asked then into the early morning if he would be someone who would call me *Ma-Ma*.

Later that day a nurse would manipulate his footprints to certify his birth somewhere in an upper-floor ward of the city that heard my midnight cry after several sweeps around Hingham Bay and candlelight dinner at the Ritz.

## 12

Zing Yang had already left on a diplomatic passport for Chongqing, the GMT's wartime capital. Anticipating the end of the war, the government had asked him to return to China to participate in the country's post-war reconstruction plans. Already a team of fifty engineers had been sent to Denver to work with the U.S. Corps of Engineers on designing a high dam on the middle of the Long River that would provide energy for the anticipated industrial needs.

There were still a few policy makers left in Chongqing who knew Zing Yang's work when he was president of Fudan University and familiar with his blueprint for institutionalizing the professional and intellectual classes, developing a national educational system that would attempt to democratize the country, making it possible for people to be mobile between classes, codifying a legal system for property and personal rights, and supporting a representational government.

Yahli and I would join him as soon as we finished tying up our affairs in Cambridge. I felt no hurry, fearful of bringing a baby into a war zone. But I was not about to let that fear overwhelm and supercede what needed to be decided and what needed to be done here and now with determination and strength—there will be plenty of time later to worry.

While I could still carry him in one arm, Yahli was almost nineteen pounds now and spending most of each day smiling and talking to the colored toy I had tied to his Swedish baby basket, a present from Shiung Chien. I first made reservations for us on the *S.S. Manhattan* to return by way of the Atlantic, but changed them to the *R.M.S. Empress of Canada*, believing the Pacific would be safer.

The agents from the Canadian Pacific Railway were most helpful, seeing us off in Boston and helping our transfer in Montréal to Vancouver, bags and all, leaving me relaxed and marveling at the panoramic vistas of the Canadian Rockies and Yahli making friends with every passerby. The sleeping car even provided a small kitchen with gas and refrigerator, making it so much easier to prepare his meals.

I was very happy he continued making friends on the ocean liner. But soon questions surfaced when several English missionaries introduced themselves to us on the open deck, the whole lot of us sailing to disembark at Shanghai. Speechless, I was trapped on board with them within the infinite reaches of the blue-green waters. For them, it was another opportunity to save heathen souls, and for me, I was reversing the Pacific Ocean almost exactly ten years later with my baby Yahli into yet another war in this century.

# SECTION FIVE

# 1

I n small groups, we disembarked the liner anchored in the harbor for safety. I pulled Yahli's hood over his head to keep off the water's spray from the small landing craft lurching towards the wharf. The kind third-mate had volunteered to carry our suitcases to the main gate.

There, at the first intersection beyond the docks, bivouacked bayoneted-soldiers and police from everywhere stood guard against each other—the sharpened ghurkas making sure the sun was still shining on the Union Jack, United States Marines with their belted canteens, helmeted Russian troops and their long rifles, and bereted French legionnaires excavating passage for the few occasional cars through the congesting throngs of civilians going nowhere.

Beyond them, I could see the gathered green khakis of the Japanese Imperial Army facing a few tousled and overwhelmed GMT conscripts. And from that distance, they looked like the aging version of those unscrubbed youths Shiung Chien and I encountered a decade ago, waiting for their imminent slaughter, or worse, imprisonment. They had been left behind to remind anyone who cared to notice just whose country this was. Everything in sight seemed to blur into the pandemonium and steel gray sky of that day. I brought Yahli closer to my breast, remaining resolute and determined to get through these barriers.

The third-mate set down the two suitcases just outside the main gate. One hand reached for his cheek as he started to say something to me, before he shook his head and looked quickly away, instantly disappearing into the pressing throng. Prepared for this, I took a deep breath and picked up one of the suitcases, the one with clothes, while the other instantly evaporated into the crowd, just like that, gone.

With Yahli awake in one arm and the suitcase in the other, I trudged and dragged and pulled us against the surging crowd, until what seemed like an hour later I just had to stop and catch my breath and decide exactly what to do next. I set the suitcase down flat, then the smiling Yahli on it, and turned around to refocus my eyes over the bobbing heads and hats toward the next intersection to identify which troops were there and if they would point me to the airport. When I turned back, Yahli and the suitcase he was sitting on were no longer there, disappeared, vanished in that fraction of a moment.

I screamed, I shrieked, *Yahli, Yahli*. I flailed and clawed into the crowd, I pushed, I shoved, I kicked, I punched. Just as tears were beginning to collect in my eyes, a short man in a dark-blue western suit yelled into my face—bring enough money there in a day and I will get my baby back and disappeared.

# 2

My body ran until it had to walk, tired, then when the breathing slowed down, back to running again, hour after hour, out of Shanghai, out of Suzhou. It had been dark for hours by the time I banged on the heavy doors to my family home in Tai Chung.

Through the crack a light came on, then the image of Ah San, the ever-faithful Ah San happy to see me, still guarding and sweeping the house even though by now its absentee father had not been seen in years and his wife too had moved elsewhere when the war and the bombing and the shelling started. When I blurted out something about my baby, kidnapped, ransom, she became very calm and serious and sat me down with a cup of tea from somewhere back in the kitchen.

Then she led me to her small cubicle in the back storeroom, lifted the blanket and mattress, pried open a loose floorboard underneath and reached into the darkness. Carefully unfolding the rough, red silk, she opened the wrapping and handed it to me with both hands. There were a handful of silver ingots, some American twenty-dollar bills, and a few small gold pieces, some I recognized, but most from what she had secreted away or stolen or earned in a lifetime, or perhaps longer.

She gave all of that to me, even though my family had given her nothing in return for an entire lifetime of dedicated and faithful service, a slave's lifetime. She gave all of that to me, for my baby, she said, because she did not have one.

## 3

Running and walking and those steps in between returning to yesterday's intersection in the skyless early morning before the sun came up to make everything in Shanghai steel-gray again, I talked to myself over and over again. What if that short man with the dark-blue western suit was not there? Did I have a choice? Who could I call on for help? Finally I decided that they would not want a baby, another mouth to feed, that they would want the silver and gold at a time when paper money had become absolutely worthless. My Yahli, my Yahli.

But he was there lurking and waiting in the crowd, looking furtively about as I handed him Ah San's silver and gold, as if we were being watched. Is that all, he asked, and pointed to the silver gray-willow pin showing underneath my coat.

When Yahli was returned to me, he looked disturbed and hungry. When I pressed him close, his heart to mine, he started smiling. At that point I decided I would avoid the contested airport and railway, and negotiate our way to Chongqing with the American twenty-dollar bills still tucked inside my panties.

Much later, Yahli would remember the next sequence in a dream. After this incident my mother changed her name and went underground. She did not take a military C-46 or C-47 to Chongqing along with escaping DPs and Madame Chiang Kaishek's Steinway CD. We traveled at night, rode in vegetable carts, each day taking small chunks out of the 1,500 miles that followed the Long River to Chongqing. During the day we sought shelter in monasteries and caves, spreading our only blanket on the ground to stay off the dampness, and evaded the soldiers on constant march on that singular narrow road edged high into the gorge over the green shallows of the river. Even at night we avoided the civilians rich enough to have a reason to go somewhere. I imagine one day I will stay in one place long enough to tell my children what happened here, until its meaning become as clear as an echo returning and embracing us all in its retelling.

## 4

**Y**es, it was true, what the graduate students warned me at Berkeley. Professor Kwok had a prearranged wife in Shantou when he was fifteen, a marriage later annulled. But not before they had three children in quick succession. They were five to eight years younger than I, and that was another reason Zing Yang had returned early, to make arrangements for their safe passage to live with us in Chongqing during the war. The oldest, who Zing Yang had stigmatized for life in naming him William James, was accompanied by his recent bride Perpetua, a smart woman who had just completed her medical studies before the outbreak of war.

> October 18, 1942
> My dear Shiung Chien,
> We live in the country, fifty miles from Chongqing,
> so we are not afraid of the air raids which everyone thinks
> will come soon. This villa is near the war-relocated Fudan
> University where Professor Kwok the pirate still knows
> many faculty members and administrators. It is easy for
> us to get our mail there and the agriculture department's
> supply for Yahli, fruit, vegetables and the goat milk that he
> dislikes.
> We are anticipating a wet but mild winter, and it is a
> comfort to be past the summer's many flies and mosquitoes.
> There were so many we took out the glass of the windows
> of the house and nailed on cloth screens because it was
> impossible to find any made out of metal. Even the cloth
> was expensive, like everything else, its price more than ten
> times than before the war. Manufactured goods are beyond
> anyone's ability to buy, even with American dollars. But we

have enough food, though limited in variety. For that we are very thankful.

Yahli is very active and talks all the time. He is acquiring a mixed vocabulary, speaking Mandarin with me, English with his father, and some strange mixture of both with the others in the house around him.

Two days a week I work at the center for children orphaned by the war. There we look after their basic needs as much as possible, and try to provide an education as well.

We are living at a very primitive level, getting up very early and going to bed early too. We cannot do anything at night because our vegetable-oil lamps do not produce much light.

Everyone in this war capital thinks the war will last at least for another two years. I don't know how they know that, but everyone seems ready to face it.

Please write me often.

Affectionately,

Your friend Katherine

5

Years from now Yahli would try to gather evidence for this period of his life in Chongqing. His nights will hum with long-distance telephone calls. He will make contact with the secretary of immigration, the archivist of birth records, the Berkeley registrar. He will pour over maps and old driving records, interview postal carriers, tricksters, insurance carriers, and even try to break into the Mormon Redemption Center. He will look up every taxonomy and geography, and collect everything tangible on both sides of the Pacific.

I will help him out here, my son thrust from my thighs and floating out there, a distant star to bring back home in this timewalk, even when in this very moment of the autobiography we were together in Chongqing. So, in the late summer of 1943, the Long River wrecked its annual havoc on the inhabitants living along its shores. Yahli had just turned four, and we were crossing the river at the height of its flood. There in the middle of the river as flotsam, branches and logs and pieces of lumber, a dead chicken, bloated goat, carried a sucking dark smell that the wind and the brown current would not dissipate.

Shouting at another boat that had turned over upstream from ours, our boatman steered us there to scavenge the planking drifting down river from the fast sinking sampan. From the opposite end of ours, Zing Yang stood up dangerously and threatened to knock him over with an oar unless he helped the drowning victims of the boat in that swift water. By then Yahli was crying and shivering and held onto my hand for comfort, while we both kept an anxious eye on the diminishing, closest shore. But the voices of Zing Yang and the boatman—shouting, cursing, threatening—made the crest of the opposite shore tilt ever so steeper as the two of them pitched back and forth, both boats sweeping downriver out of control.

6.

*T*his next happened in 1943, *as Yahli was to write much later, probably well into autumn, at least several months after the Long River's flooding had receded. The war must have started turning around for Chiang Kaishek—past the heavy wooden gates of our villa, endless columns of GMT troops were daily marching towards the coast on the road parallel to the river. Breaking the monotonous clanging of their mess kits, stirred the occasional low whirring hum of a staff car with its unit chevron, or a diesel truck, its canvas flap concealing what was inside.*

*But mostly there were hundreds and thousands of soldiers moving at the same speed as the vehicles, their uniform the exact ordinary color as the road dust they stirred. Some of them did not have rifles, and I remember my half brother William James saying that some of the others did not have any ammunition. One or two of their faces would always be turned up towards where I was watching them from the top step in front of the gates. Ma-Ma told me I had to keep the gates closed. I was four that summer, and lowered the thick, wooden bar as I was told.*

*That was also the summer I learned about cicadas and departures of another kind. William had a highly prized bamboo stick at least twelve or fifteen feet long, and he taught me how to catch cicadas with it. First he would show me by example, then he would stand behind me and help me as I was tested before I was allowed on my own, even when he was not watching.*

*We would first slowly twist the tip of the stick around some spider webs in crevices around the house and the wall that surrounded the house until the tip was crested and darkened with the sticky cobweb. When he was helping me, there were four hands on the stick turning it in unison, and I remember feeling a sense of purposefulness in that combination. Occasionally he would ask me to let go of the stick so that he could reach higher under the roof's eaves.*

*Finding the cicadas was easy. We stood still and listened. It seemed in that summer the steady stridulation. of a high pitched resonance was always in the air. Even today when every other noise is down in my life, my inner ear can still hear that continuous sound, the electrical strike of cicadas at first contact. We listened for breaks in that sound, a short but sustained grinding note repeated again and again, and followed it to the small darkish lumps on tree branches silhouetted against the clear skies of Chongqing.*

*The delicate movement of surprising the cicadas from below and behind was the most difficult technique to learn. It had to be done slowly, so the insect would not be frightened off, but not so slowly to allow its escape. I now suspect the truthfulness of this part of William's instruction as much as his report about the soldiers' ammunition supply. Once I mustered enough strength to control the quivering of the stick's tip fifteen feet up and made contact, the cicada was doomed.*

*What I don't remember now is what exactly we did with the cicadas afterwards. I imagine that William probably had a little stick cage to harbor them, or a matchbox, in which he kept alive our collection with daily ablutions of water. We would lift it once in a while, shake it, expecting to stimulate ethereal song from the captured cicadas.*

*This was the summer of my earliest recollection; and it has been held captive until now in these unspoken and inescapable images. This was also the summer that Will, being married to Perpetua at the time, had slipped into the bed of a servant one night and was henceforth banished forever into a cage of his own making.*

7

When the war appeared to be turning around, Zing Yang was spending more and more time in Chongqing. My cough was getting worse, but I tried not to show it, not even when some spotting appeared in my handkerchief.

> March 21, 1944
> My dear Shiung Chien,
> The people are beginning to look up, now that the U.S. has entered the war against Japan. Their faces appear hopeful. Professor Kwok the pirate is spending more and more time in the capital making plans for the post-war reconstruction.
> It seems strange that I am addressing my letter to you in Box 1663. How large is this box? Do you live in this box and work somewhere else? You mentioned in your letter that you are working on a gadget. Is that a toy of some kind? I hope it is not taking time away from your Nobel-bound research on weak interactions and parity symmetry breaking.
> Yahli is very happy and growing rapidly.
> We are all anticipating the end of the war soon.
> Affectionately,
> Your lasting friend, Katherine

Later that spring, Zing Yang started bringing home giant, red tomatoes from Fudan's agriculture department. He would immerse his hands into a white, porcelain bowl and squeeze out their juice telling me that I should drink it, I should drink it, it will be good for me, like blood in the burgeoning quarter moon.

## 8

*It is difficult now to imagine I was in the middle of events that changed the lives of close to one billion people, but to a child then, their significance held no portent. Surely the sunlight must have moved shadows behind trees and buildings that autumn, and just as surely someone must have recorded that moment in a journal or a letter. But what happened in fact in one short moment that autumn early evening some forty-four years and six thousand miles from the here and now—the single event that must have touched me but has through the years been held in denial, however catastrophic, ordinary or benign, its continuum breaking down into disconnected fragments, each with its own urgent tedium to attend to—has escaped history, its memory privileged, locked away and wordless.*

*But since memory is also inventive, it can now begin realigning what happened in that one moment in the past and allow me to walk away from its significant rubble with something of my own. This then is the prodigal hand forever reaching out, mending. This will not be the story that has been left behind.*

I was propped up on pillows that early evening, and only Yahli seemed to have been in the house in another room, all else quiet in the diminishing light. I knew no grief and no pain and understood the need to whisper, year after year and anticipate the silence that will follow.

Yahli walked alone into the room, hesitant, but he followed his steps right up to the bedside, his eyes and hand touching mine. I felt my presence ebbing away, my name changing, and agreed to it, in the last moment feeling bound to him with a living hand from afar.

# SECTION SIX

1

There must have been a funeral—I do not remember it exactly, only the silence that trailed it. The immediate past future is very hazy, and some blank pages followed. Yet over the years sometimes I hear my voice shifting ever so slightly above the hum of that summer. Under my eyelids I can still see the pagodas perched high in the rim above the gorge of that rampaging river in my sleep, the tiny monks sequestered from the roily din below, the blanket laid down against the ground's dampness.

The five of them then—Zing Yang, Perpetua, the remaining other two half-siblings and Yahli—moved at different times in the roped cargo hold of a military C-46 or a C-47 to Shanghai in the spring of 1945. The end of the war must have been in sight, and preparations must have been under way for moving Fudan University back to Shanghai. More people appeared and just as suddenly disappeared in Yahli's life.

Occasionally the air raid sirens would scream at night and sometimes the electric lights would go off. But mostly someone would switch off the lights, and Yahli would follow instructions and obediently hide under the dining room table. There were a few indiscriminate bombs, some shaking windows, and in the mornings after the street vendors would hawk the night's parachuted supply of powder milk and Hersey chocolates to the highest bidder.

Yahli's half-brother and half-sister disappeared, returned to their graduate studies he would learn much later. He played with the light switches, making sure each one in the apartment worked. Perpetua said his fingernails were too long, but he did not let her trim them.

He learned to find his own moments by getting up before everyone else in the morning. He would walk around the apartment looking into everything, and once placed his hand under his sleeping father's nose to see if he were alive.

In the unbroken silence of one such morning in early August, he saw an unearthly blue light throbbing in the distant sky beyond the east window, as if the sun for just a few seconds had been displaced by a pale, blue sheen covering everything. By the time he got to the window for a better look, it had disappeared.

# 2

By the time the Instruments of Surrender had been signed by both sides on the *U.S. Missouri* anchored in Tokyo Bay on the second morning of September, it had become increasingly clear to Zing Yang that his vision for a post-war reconstruction program for China was not going to work within the GMT's floundering bureaucracies and competing self interests.

Furthermore, while the nation stumbled out of the war with Japan with a staggering twenty million dead, it was immediately followed by a total collapse of the economy, accompanied by an extensive famine affecting just about every region of the country. The country under perpetual siege, random collective acts swelled in conspicuous violence and exploitation, shrilled, roared, and, hooved in scaffold, everywhere ran, crowing, day and night, lives lost in essential lies and contingency lies, ideology and metaphor abandoned, huddled between betrayal and survival. Above all of these calamities, there was the major issue of the unfinished civil war with Mao Zedong, whose political projections were not clear to Zing Yang, though he had his suspicions, given his limited access to Mao's thinking.

At this point he decided to sideline himself from these developments, at least for the moment, and move to neutral turf where he would wait and see. So within the year he collected what was left of his quickly dispersing family, gathered as much left of personal possessions that he could exchange into American dollars, and moved the three of them—himself, Yahli, and his daughter-in-law Perpetua of his errant and banished son—south to the British Crown Colony of Hong Kong.

3

To counter war's dislocation and its fracturing impact on families, then, Zing Yang and Perpetua talked deep into the night. They pulled their remaining things together, to start afresh by lowering the curtain on the past, to make things normal again, to move to a country where new neighbors and new friends will not ask about our past and we will not tell. There will be an unarticulated, mutual agreement that certain things will not be talked about: politics, religion and family history.

Perpetua and Zing Yang will pass themselves off as a married couple—a father and a mother, and Yahli will be their son, although at the beginning he insisted he already had a mother. That is, Zing Yang's former daughter-in-law Perpetua will acquire an additional hyphen for her identity and become his ex-daughter-in-law, morphing instantly into his wife in one declarative sentence. They believed this would be the most universally accepted model of identity, the *family*, and no stigma would be attached to this DP! And nothing more was said. Their life will henceforth begin in 1947, in Hong Kong. And nothing more was to be said, at all, ever, and much less than nothing to think about.

This has been a common narrative in the twentieth century for hundreds of millions of DPs, victims of cataclysmic upheavals, for someone we know personally, or someone known by someone we know personally. When we look hard enough, there is always a gap of years missing in everyone's family history. The perpetrator and the victim alike, they live in houses inhabited by the same silence.

Perpetual war, followed by pathological silence. Many have come down this stream before, and often the results have been painful and destructive. Did they live in fear that their past denied would one unexpected day catch up and cripple them?

4

For Perpetua, Yahli's new "stepmother," finding a position as a general practitioner in Hong Kong was relatively easy, an appointment in Kowloon Hospital. It was more difficult for her trying to keep up the big lie, with her nephew-now-son living in the same house. She and Zing Yang were never married legally, not in Shanghai, and not in Hong Kong—a self-declared marriage.

After Zing Yang had passed away, his lips sealed shut forever, Perpetua was to explain to Yahli that he later reported in another narrative, *We were the only ones left at the end of the war, she explained to me when I asked her over the phone some fifty years later why they never got married. We started to live together for survival.*

*We were the only ones left, she repeated at the end of the phone call.*

*Later she would write to tell me that I should have asked my father while he was still around, as she put it. Two years later she wrote again.*

*My friends tell me you are going to China to teach linguistics. Why haven't you told me? Will you be teaching in Chinese?*

*And then another letter waited for me when I arrived in Beijing. What is linguistics? Does the AMA approve of it? Have you regained your proficiency in speaking Chinese, especially Mandarin?*

*Strange, coming from someone who would only speak to me in Shanghai-wa in all those eight years I was in Hong Kong, while she spoke English to everyone else she knew, even when sometimes the only words they understood were* okay, bye-bye *and* fuck. *Now she speaks to me in English only, when she speaks to me at all.*

For almost twenty years, Perpetua urged Yahli to go into a science, or get a M.D., or at least a Ph.D., finally giving up when he was appointed the academic vice chancellor of the University of Colorado without any of them.

*One early Sunday morning she had a severe accident driving on the L.A.*

*freeway by herself, and she called to tell me about it. Then ten minutes after we hung up, she called again and wanted to know what I was doing awake at three in the morning. She called a week later at two in the morning and wanted me to take the typhoid shot.*

*That's good. You called to tell me that? D'you know what time it is here?*

*Yes, yes, of course. It's only a rumor. It's not useful. There's plenty of time for diagnosis and treatment; there's no need for any gene-tricking immunization, not even the oral type.*

*I just had to ask it then. How're you doing?*

*Fine. The photo you sent standing in front of Genghis Khan's birth yurt when you went to Hohhot—you are wrong! You are believing too many commercials again. Look closely. There are wheels under the yurt. It's off a movie set.*

In telling this story later, Yahli was beginning to discover that he had never liked her, Perpetua, the survivor.

5

For Zing Yang, however, his employment chances diminished quickly when he discovered that the institution that would welcome someone like him with his credentials, experience, publications, and research agenda, the University of Hong Kong had in place an apartheid policy of not hiring any Chinese. With his wife Perpetua's promising medical career in the balance, he decided to stay and not move again. Eleven times in nine years was enough. Time to pull back and reassess who he was, what was important to him, and what realistic professional options were still available to him.

With the outbreak of the Korean War and Senator McCarthy looking for scapegoats with the revitalized House Un-American Activities Committee, Zing Yang started pacing the floor of our apartment in his slippers from morning to night. From the veranda through the living room and into their bedroom and his study and then in reverse, a cup of chrysanthemum tea forever sitting on his writing desk, maybe the same one from the day before or the week before. Occasionally he would pause in front of his desk and picking up the always-opened pen, he would jot down a word, a phrase or sometimes an entire sentence.

By the time President Truman relieved General MacArthur of his Korean command, Hong Kong was going through its own internal upheavals. Chairman Mao Zedong's declaration of the success of the Communists in Beijing in 1949 had lead to the massive exodus of Chinese intellectuals and professionals into Taiwan and Hong Kong, doubling and tripling and quadrupling its population in just a few years.

But many of them in Hong Kong were not so lucky, as agents of both the Guomintang in Taipei and Chinese Communist Party in Beijing arrived weekly and carried out targeted killings against them—retaliation for acts committed in the past, betrayals, rejection of invitations to join, and pre-empting their defection to the other side. Some of them would occasionally stop at their apartment, and in ones or twos behind the living room's closed double doors, they would talk in whispers, once in a while a raised voice, but always below the level of my eavesdropping. This went on for one, maybe two years, the British police finally giving up on their futile attempts to catch the perpetrators or stop the assignations altogether.

Zing Yang never appeared anxious during this period, and somehow he was not even scratched by a warning bullet or a threatening blade. Maybe it was true, he did save Zhou Enlai's life in 1927 Shanghai, and the Generalissimo Cash-My-Check was from his same Fujian Province, after all. Maybe both sides were just holding out, leaving open the opportunity for him to join.

My Yahli would learn decades later that during this interval Zing Yang was receiving huge grants from various American sources—academic journals of sociology, social psychology, Asia Foundation, Human Ecology Fund, to conduct exit interviews with the mainland Chinese escaping into Hong Kong, much in the same way that Hadley Cantril, head of Princeton University's psychology department at the time, was carrying out the same kind of interviews with exiting eastern Europeans. These funding organizations were cover for the Central Intelligence Agency's contracted clandestine intelligence gathering of data from countries behind the Iron and Bamboo Curtains, another instance in which the self-serving perception of autonomy and independence of scientific research was compromised and surrendered to the nation's political agenda in the name of homeland security.

Zing Yang was entering these interviews into the manuscript he was working on, *Confessions of a Chinese Scientist*, making purple carbon copies to be couriered by Star Ferry to the American Consulate across the harbor, these briefing papers that attempted to profile the political and cultural climate of China's interior.

When Yahli was going through Professor Kwok the pirate's papers after his death some seventeen years later, he found his last, unpublished book manuscript. Tucked into its pages was a stamped envelope with my hand writing that he recognized instantly. It was my last letter, addressed to my friend Shiung Chien Wu at Box 1663, Santa Fe, New Mexico, who must have been in Los Alamos working on the Manhattan Project, a.k.a. the Buck Rogers Project. Zing Yang had never mailed this letter from

Chongqing, but had kept it all these years, maybe the only thing of mine he could keep, even when it was not intended for him.

6

In 1955 Yahli embarked on a Maru liner for Brooklyn with his baseball mitt and olive-green American passport, with calls at Yokohama, San Pedro, through the locks of the Panama Canal, and then Charleston. Somewhere out there is a snapshot of Zing Yang saying his very last good-bye to him. In the picture he is standing on the ship's fore-deck, his right hand shading his eyes from the sun, Kowloon's purple-green nine-dragoned hills in the background. It was a reverse voyage for Yahli. What he did not know until this writing, it was also a reverse voyage for me, back across the Pacific Ocean, and back across time.

By now it should be evident that it takes more than one person to write an autobiography, that for an autobiography to have any authenticity and hence value, it must extend beyond just one generation. In the case of my autobiography, my son has participated in its writing, mother and son, son and mother, traversing timewalks, investigating concealed narratives, discovering meaning in gaps in this common twentieth century narrative of significance to people on both sides of the Pacific.

We have been told that there are more than eleven dimensions, though most of us are only familiar with three, or at most four. What lies beyond can only be explained to those interested in mathematical models, analogies, metaphors and paradoxes, and some of these are folded within each other. Mostly what we can conceptualize is based on what we know within the basic three-four dimensions. Take this norm away, and it's blank, an absolute zero.

But within this norm that we live in from day to day, we must make the occasional allowance and suspend its limits, and for maybe a moment trust what the fictions have to offer us. Maybe just another chance of whatever significance, but nevertheless a chance. It is not that difficult to be two persons.

For me, these words have given me back my life, my life in his time. Before this, I had existed only in unsubstantiated memories. But in the writing now I can stand up and talk and be who I am and what I am. And my last words in my biography will then be tucked into the first words of his autobiography.

*Sixty years ago this was my universe where I lived and played, mostly by myself. Now I was back as an impatient and sweaty tourist from another postcolonial country some three thousand miles away bursting in air, as if I was late for a meeting, a bumpy voice recorder hitched to my waist. Despite the massive land use alterations resulting from the political reclamation and entrepreneurial ventures, actually I knew exactly where I was, headed home via a series of diagonal crossings and trespassing shortcuts. Or more correctly, where home was, in the last apartment building on that hill, there on a short street ending at the backside of the Royal Observatory where its seasonal typhoon signals were visible to every mariner in the harbor of this crown colony under King George VI, Number Ten being the severest.*

*Most of the old buildings had disappeared, and the vegetation as well, including the expansive banyan trees, now replaced by an occasional bauhinia bush planted to reverse the racial and political hegemony. Though I may not have known exactly who I was at that jostled moment, I knew precisely where I was in time, and I was in a hurry. Here, the Chanticleer bakery with its fresh, creamy napoleons across the street from the resident Argyle and most-feared Gurkha barracks, next the comics book stand, both temptations on the walk home from the Immaculate Conception elementary school where I learned to tuck slide into second base, demonstrated one recess by an eager nun in flowing white habit.*

*Here the trek was interrupted by a residential development of infinite small houses, each with its narrow stone steps leading to doors of equally colorless homes, except for their sky-blue trim. Several men suddenly appeared, including one who looked Indian or Pakistani, even though his skin was too light. They wanted to know what I was looking for, Torpedo Alley, they called their neighborhood in Chinese without smiling. But I knew better, they were fooling me, looking at the harbor some two hundred feet in elevation below us. It was clear they did not want me there, now as well as sixty years ago. So I explained that as a writer I was not balanced, I had just lost my way to the ferry terminal. The Indian or Pakistani man said he understood, since his wife was also a writer, of novels, he said, his eyes still a patch of doubt, and pointed, downhill first, then to the right.*

*Clutching my recorder then, I went downhill first, but once out of their sight around the next corner, I turned onto a muddy field where several pages were missing. Gone were the small houses and concrete sidewalk. Instead, sparse vegetable plots garnished the landscape from edge to edge. Two men in their thirties came up from one of them, though I knew they were really in their eighties, because as witness I could identify them, coming around every afternoon collecting metal, glass or paper they'd sell for recycling, rain or shine.*

*One of them pointed down to a row of garlic stems by his feet and said it was his. He directed his finger to the next row and said these fat cabbages were his friend's. Then he said the last row of tiny, dark green bitter melons belonged to both of them, tendered most carefully, even in the wet and windy summer typhoon season, to keep them from rotting, he added at the end as I continued downhill to the ferry terminal.*

*By this time the men from Torpedo Alley had caught up with me and my transformational tricks in hallucination or dream. Like their security predecessors, they scolded me and escorted me to the gate, just when I was perfectly balanced on a high banyan limb. I used to live near here, some sixty years ago, I was sure of it.*

*Look here, at the Star Ferry terminal then, I skip the Morning Star and the Meridian Star and wait for the Celestial Star for the crossing. In my hands the recorder clutch the words most dear to those missing pages for which I live on my way home.*

Photo by Zoe Filipkowska

## AUTHOR BIO

Alex Kuo has been an administrator and a teacher of writing, literature, ethnic and cultural studies at several American universities. He has also taught writing, translation and American literature in Chinese universities.

He has three National Endowment for the Arts awards, and grants from the Bureau of Indian Affairs, the United Nations, Artist Trust, and the Idaho, Pennsylvania and Washington state arts organizations. He has been awarded a Senior Fulbright, a Lingnan, and a Rockefeller Foundation Bellagio residency. He has also held the positions of Writer-in-Residence for Mercy Corps and the Distinguished Writer-in-Residence at Knox College. In 2008 he was invited to be the Distinguished Writer-in-Residence at Shanghai's Fudan University.

More than three hundred-and-fifty of his poems, short stories, photographs and essays have appeared in magazines and newspapers. His most recent books are *This Fierce Geography* (poems/1999), *Lipstick and Other Stories* (2001) which received the 2002 American Book Award, and *Panda Diaries* (novel/2006).

www.alexkuo.org

For other Wordcraft of Oregon, LLC,
titles, please visit our website at:

www.wordcraftoforegon.com

Printed in the United States
125889LV00010B/113/P

9 781877 655616